Jericho

Rigby Brothers, Volume 6

S L Davies

Published by S L Davies, 2022.

JERICHO

First edition. October 19, 2022.

Copyright © 2022 S L Davies.

ISBN: 979-8215527009

Written by S L Davies.

Prologue

J ericho

"What did he want with the valkyrie child anyway?" I asked my brother Bacchus as we sat out the back of his house, sipping on beers and watching the kids run about playing. We'd been called out to a fire that afternoon at the Onyx Rebels headquarters. The fire had been set by Ettore, a Nephilim who was rumored to be controlling a war and running a lot of breeding facilities.

Everything I'd learned about Ettore made me hate him even more. But when I'd seen one of the Onyx Rebels members kicking the shit out of the demon while a little girl screamed for her mother, I realized just how dangerous Ettore was.

"Hildr is a mighty girl, she can transport psychically both in sleep and awake, plus she can converse with the valkyrie goddess Hel," Bacchus explained.

My eyes widened, and my mouth dropped open. "Seriously? These kids of this generation are fucking something else."

"You can say that again. I'm grateful that Butler stopped that fucker from taking her away."

I nodded as I thought about what would have happened if Ettore had gotten hold of Iver. The war terrified me. I couldn't imagine what Anghus, Bacchus, and Joachim would do; they would burn the entire world down to get him back. Ettore terrified me. I hated him, but I feared him too.

I stroked my hand down over my beard and groaned, stretching in my chair. "This is too fucking much."

Bacchus yawned and stretched, scratching at his chest. "You're telling me. I'm exhausted and worried. I want to go in and just kill Ettore immediately. But that fucker is so slippery it is almost impossible."

"How many facilities has he got left?"

"I can't say for sure. We didn't know about the Fowlers Gap facility until we were involved in shutting it down. But there are five that we know for sure about. That's not including the one he has in the underworld or the training center."

"Jesus. Where are the other five?" I couldn't believe he had gotten away with something like this for so long. I'd met several of the omegas rescued from the breeding facilities through the Devil's Advocates. What they had been through was nothing short of a horror story.

"There is one in South Africa, two in Japan, one in New Zealand, and one on Pitcairn Island."

"Shit," I swore. If they were all over the world, it meant that Kade didn't have the authority to go in and shut them down. I remembered what it was like for Bacchus and Anghus while they planned to go to Siberia. It had taken months of research and working with governments.

"Yep. I don't think the Japanese facilities will be open for much longer. Kade has been in contact with the Japanese government, and they were furious about it. I'm not sure if we will be involved in shutting them down, but I think now that the government bodies know about it, they will do something."

I nodded my head and took another swig of my beer. "What about the others? Is Kade talking to those governments?"

Bacchus nodded his head. "Yep. So far, the New Zealand government is blowing us off and doesn't seem to care. South Africa has just said they need to investigate it but seem to be dragging their feet."

"Do you reckon that New Zealand is doing shady shit with Ettore, and that's why they don't care?"

Bacchus shrugged his shoulders. "I don't know. It could be that. But I think it's possibly out of sight, out of mind. If no one important is being affected, they don't care. New Zealand seems to be a little bit behind in its ways of accepting supernaturals. A huge part of the human population still doesn't accept supernaturals as equals over there."

I shook my head and sighed. "It's fucked. How long do we have to exist before they know we aren't going anywhere?"

Bacchus chuckled. "Yeah, we've been around even fucking longer than humans. But it is what it is. Nothing we can do about it."

I scrubbed my hand up over my face and closed my eyes. The sun's warmth soaked into my skin, and my dragon sat close to the surface, warming his body and enjoying the day off. It felt like it'd been forever since I'd taken a day off. I'd been working steadily, and with Ettore causing issues all over Lalbert, there seemed to be more call-outs than usual.

"We will end him one day," I said, glancing over at Bacchus.

"We sure will. Iver will be thirteen years old in a couple of weeks; time is moving fast. It scares me, but I've got to accept it."

Time had moved so quickly. It felt like only yesterday that Bacchus had met Anghus and Joachim.

"How do you think Anghus and Joachim will feel when the time comes for Iver to fight?"

Bacchus shrugged, and I could see the sadness on his face as I looked at him. "It's going to tear their hearts out. But it is part of the prophecy; there isn't any other way around it without letting Ettore win."

"I will be fighting by his side."

"Me too, brother."

Chapter One

F lame
Eric was in the worst mood I'd ever seen him in. He had already killed five demons and didn't look like he would slow down anytime soon. It was the first time I'd seen him lose his shit. I didn't quite understand what was happening, but I knew something terrible had happened.

"This is fucked; that cunt needs to fucking die. I asked you to do one fucking thing. One thing, grab the child and bring her back here. But you couldn't even do that," Eric snarled into the face of the demon he was dressing down.

Lux looked thoroughly chagrined as he bowed his head and stood before Eric. "I'm sorry. I never expected that they would have a demon Nephilim there."

Eric sighed and scrubbed his hands up over his face. "Morrigan. I should have never trusted that asshole all those years ago. They have done nothing but cause me trouble." Eric turned and spotted me standing in the corner. I'd tried to get out of the room when Eric had first entered, but he'd stood in front of the door, and I'd been trapped.

"What is your name?" he asked.

"Flame," I responded quietly.

Eric nodded and glanced over at Lux before looking back at me. "I have a job for you."

My stomach began to riot with nerves. I didn't know what he would expect of me, but it couldn't be anything good. Nothing Eric did was good. I'd been bred and raised in this facility and didn't know anything else. I'd tried to escape since I was a child, but somehow Eric always knew, and I was captured.

My body was dotted with scars that had been caused by him. I lifted my fingers to my cheek, where the most recent scar crossed over. He'd almost taken my eye out as he slashed me with the machete. And now he looked at me like he didn't know me.

"Ettore," Lux said. "That's Flame, the omega that keeps trying to escape."

Ettore? I didn't know this name. Eric turned to face Lux before he turned his glare on me. "How long ago did you last try to escape?"

"A year ago," I answered quietly. It wasn't that I'd learned my lesson; it was that the wound Eric had caused to my face last time had been so bad that I was afraid of what would happen if I tried it again.

Eric nodded his head. "If you do this job for me, I will allow you to go free," he said with a smile.

His smile said he was telling the truth, but it was in his eyes that the lie was held. He was full of shit. I knew it didn't matter what I did; I'd never truly be free from here. He would either always pull me back or he would kill me. It would only be in death; I'd be free, and even then, I wondered if that was the case.

"I'll do the job," I said quietly. It wasn't like I had a choice anyway. Even if I didn't want to do the job, which I certainly didn't, I knew he wouldn't give me a choice.

"Good answer," Eric smirked.

He stepped toward me. Lux sighed and scrubbed his hands over his face. I could tell he disagreed with Eric's decision to use me for whatever job Lux had failed him. But Eric's mind was made up; I wouldn't be given a choice.

When Eric was standing before me, he looked down into my face. Gently he brought his fingers up to my cheek and skimmed them along the scar. I shuddered at the feel of his ice-cold fingers on my skin. Fear settled in my stomach. This man was evil incarnate. There was not an ounce of good in him. If there was a devil, Eric was it.

"You are going to go and get me the valkyrie child and bring her back here," he said. His voice held a gravel quality that made my anxiety spike.

"Where is the child?" I asked.

"She is the daughter of the Onyx Rebel member. This child has the powers of Hel, and I need her here." I nodded my head as Eric stared into my eyes. I couldn't believe I was going to do this. Kidnapping. For fucks sake, was I really going to go this low. Suddenly Eric pressed his fingers to my forehead, and images of a little girl with white hair and eyes filled my mind. She was curled up on her mother's lap with her thumb in her mouth. When Eric removed his fingers from my forehead, I gasped for air.

"Do this job, and I will let you be free," he said with a smirk.

"No, you won't," I said with a sigh and shake of my head. "But I'll do it for you."

Eric tapped my cheek with the palm of his hand. "Good boy. There is a reason you were always my favorite."

I raised my brow as I looked up into Eric's face. Only a matter of moments ago he was asking my name and acting like he didn't remember me. I wondered if that was all a charade. I wouldn't be surprised. Eric was something different to anyone else I'd ever met. He was dangerously intelligent and unpredictable. He was the worst kind of villain.

Chapter Two

Jericho

"How bad was the damage?" I asked our chief Marlan. He leaned back in his chair and rubbed his hands over his face.

"Bad. Ettore used hellfire to burn the place; it decimated the buildings."

"Shit," I said with a wince. We had to report the mess that Ettore had caused at the Onyx Rebels headquarters. Butler had been burned and was still in hospital, but from all accounts, his body was healing well. I was only grateful that no one was too severely injured.

"Yeah. That fucker is getting too close for comfort. I'm worried about what is going to happen next. He is becoming unhinged."

I nodded my head and leaned back in the chair opposite Marlan. "That's what is worrying me. I'm scared for my nephew and nieces."

Marlan nodded. "Me too. This is just too fucking much."

"What has Kade said about it all?"

"He is furious, as you can well imagine. He said he is preparing for more problems; I won't be surprised."

"Can't they arrest him now?"

"They must be able to get a hold of him long enough to arrest him. He is a sneaky bastard."

"Yeah, I guess that's why he has managed to evade capture for so long."

"Yep. Worse, he has facilities that even the AJE authority didn't know about."

My eyes widened, and I gasped. "Holy shit. How many more?"

Marlan shrugged his shoulders. "No idea. But the one that they shut down that sparked all of this they didn't know about until a few days before they raided."

I groaned and thrust my hands up into my hair. "Fuck I hate him."

"You're preaching to the converted with that."

My phone started to ring, and I glanced down to see that it was Bacchus calling. "Hey, big brother, what's up?"

"We have a problem."

"What?" I asked, feeling worry start to float through me.

"One of the kids has been abducted."

I gasped. "Which one?" I asked as my worry morphed to panic.

"Lake, Memphis, and Ciaran's fifteen-year-old daughter," Bacchus said.

"Okay," I replied, feeling a bit of guilt bite me as relief washed over me that it wasn't one of my nephews or nieces. "Was it Ettore?"

"We think so. The school rang Memphis when she never arrived, and we discovered that she hadn't even made it as far as school."

I frowned. "And there were no witnesses?"

"I don't know. We have got Coltrane, Memphis, and Pax out there, seeing if they can pick up on her scent."

"What can I do?"

"I could use you out there searching; your powers are strong."

It was true. I was a dragon shifter alpha. I had psychic powers and strength and could see things that were only imprints.

"Alright, send me a text with the route she takes to school, and I'll head out there and see what I can pick up."

"Thank you. Arcadia and Scout are out there on it too."

"Alright, I'll take Maison with me if he is free."

"Thank you, Jericho. I'm sending the map through now," Bacchus said as I heard the message alert ring.

"Got it," I replied as I opened the file to look at the marked route that Lake usually took to school. "I'll head out there now."

"Talk soon," Bacchus said as he ended the call.

"Ettore?" Marlan asked.

"Yeah, looks that way. Memphis from the Shifter Unit, his daughter, was abducted on the way to school. Bacchus has asked me to go and see what I can pick up." The beauty of being supernatural was that we were able to work together. Marlan understood that when the AJE authority called for help, we would drop everything that wasn't an emergency to go and assist.

Marlan nodded his head. "Definitely take Maison with you then."

I nodded and jogged out of the office towards the living quarters, where Maison was sitting on the couch watching television.

"Hey, Mais, can you give us a hand. One of the AJE authority members' children was abducted this morning. I'm about to head out to the route she took to school to see what I can pick up."

Maison sat up and nodded his head. "Of course." Maison was a dragon shifter, also. In fact, all of Lalbert Fire was run by dragon shifters. A bit ironic that firefighters are dragons, known for fire, but it was what it was. Maison's powers were incredible. He was directly descended from the goddess Demeter, the one from which dragons got their powers. The first dragon Nephilim came from Demeter. And Maison was her great-great-grandson.

Maison stood from the couch and joined me. "Let's go," he said, his eyes flared orange as he called his dragon close to the surface and pulled on his powers.

Chapter Three

Flame
The screaming was soul-shattering. It echoed from every wall and hit me straight in the chest. I followed the screams until I found a girl who couldn't have been older than fifteen fighting with Lux.

"Sit down," Lux growled through clenched teeth.

"Fuck you," the girl screamed in his face. Her eyes were red with tears, and she looked like she had a large bruise forming on her cheek. Lux recoiled his hand and slapped the girl, knocking her head to the side. She glared back at Lux. "Fuck. You."

Lux growled, curling his lip over his teeth in a snarl. Magic rippled through the air, and I watched, horrified, as the girl began to morph. Her body twisted, and a roar slipped from her lips. She morphed into a giant dragon, but on her head, she had horns, and her body was that of a tiger. I'd never seen a creature like it, and I was curious. Not that I had a lot of experience with shifters. But she was unusual, and from the ripple of magic surrounding her, she was dangerous. With a speed that I couldn't even fathom, the girl's head twisted, and one of her horns had impaled through Lux's chest.

The demon's eyes widened, and he gasped. The girl pushed her head forward and slammed Lux into the wall, penetrating her horn into the wall behind him. Lux's eyes rolled in his head as his spirit left his body. Blood oozed from his chest and down over the girl's horn.

Magic rippled again when Eric suddenly appeared in the room. He stared at the girl before moving his hands. Suddenly the dragon screeched as if in pain. A wave of power washed through the room as the dragon writhed and shrunk until it had transformed back into the girl, now naked and coated in Lux's blood.

Lux's body slid down the wall unceremoniously into a pile on the floor. "Well, that's a shame; he was one of my better ones," Eric sighed with a shake before he turned his attention to the girl who was trembling on the ground. Her wide blue eyes stared up at Eric.

"Ettore," she snarled. "You are responsible for this."

Ettore again? I didn't know why people kept calling him Ettore. I wondered if it was a nickname.

Eric chuckled and rolled his eyes. "Of course I am, child. You thought someone would want your skinny ass for something other than your powers." The girl snarled but remained silent. Eric glanced around the room and spotted me standing in the corner, staring.

"Ah, what's your name again?" he asked with a smirk on his lips. His eyes were narrowed dangerously, and I could see his mind working.

"Flame," I answered quietly. Annoyance welled up inside me that he couldn't remember my name. He wanted me to kidnap a child for him but couldn't take the time to remember my name. Then again, it was quite possible that it was a ruse and Eric was just playing a game. One thing I'd learned quickly here was that you could never tell what Eric was thinking.

"That's right. Flame. Take the girl to the cells and lock her up. I'll be curious to see how long it takes before we are crawling with AJE authority and Devil's Advocates members."

"They will come after you," the girl said quietly.

Eric turned with a maniacal smile and nodded his head. "I'm counting on it."

He was preparing a trap. He was going to kill innocent people. This girl was innocent. He'd taken her to try and kill others.

"Well, come on, Flame, get to it," Eric said, snapping his fingers.

I walked over to where the girl was cowered on the floor. She watched me with wariness in her eyes. It wasn't until I was on her that I noticed the silver cuff around her throat. I didn't see when Eric had put it on her, but it was obvious why she couldn't shift back into that dragon creature to kill him or me.

"Come on," I said quietly, reaching out my hand to hers. The girl continued to stare at me but didn't move.

"For fucks sake, just grab her," Eric growled.

I sighed but reached out my hand and clasped the girl's bicep. Using my strength, I pulled her up off the ground.

"Let go of me," she snapped as she attempted to wriggle out of my hold. I wasn't a big man, but I was still taller and had more strength than the teenaged girl.

"Just walk," I growled in return, dragging her away under the watchful stare of Eric. She didn't realize how dangerous this man was and what damage he could cause. It would be much easier for her to do as she was told.

I could feel the girl trying to call on her magic, but I knew that the silver cuff had rendered her no more powerful than a human. I dragged her out of the room while she fought against my hold.

Once I was far away from Eric, I turned to face the girl. "Look, I hate him as much as you do, just do as he expects, and you won't end up being hurt."

The girl searched my face. "Why do you work for him if you hate him?"

I rolled my eyes. Like I had a choice. "I don't have any other option. See this?" I said, pointing at my cheek. The girl nodded her head. "I got that from trying to escape. All the other scars all over my body are from him too. Just do what he expects, and you might be allowed to live."

"If I have to live in this hell, I'd rather die."

I sighed and nodded my head before I started walking toward the cells once more. She had a point. Something I'd considered many times. But I was a coward. I was too afraid to die.

Chapter Four

J ericho

When Maison and I reached the house that Memphis, Ciaran, Lake, and her little sister Lilah lived in, Anghus and all the Devil's Advocates' inner crew were already there. Anghus looked over at me and gave me a small smile.

"How are they doing?" I asked as I embraced Anghus.

He sighed and shook his head. "Ciaran is beside himself and ready to burn the entire world down. Memphis is on the warpath."

I nodded my head. "This is the first time he has ever been so fucking bold," I growled. All the other times we've had an issue with Ettore, it was rescuing others. But this time, he had taken one of our own. Right after he destroyed the Onyx Rebels headquarters, he was getting brave or sloppy. I couldn't tell what it was. But he was bringing this war closer.

"Yeah. I want to fucking kill him."

"Me too. Alright, Maison and I will try and pick up on Lake's trail."

"Thanks, keep in touch; we are all in this together."

I nodded my head and clasped Anghus's arm. "Make sure you look after Iver. If Ettore gets his hands on him, then we are done."

Anghus's muscles tightened under my hand as his eyes flashed black. "I'll tear him limb from limb," he growled so deep and gravelly that it made me shiver. The gargoyle's power in him was terrifying, and I believed every word he said.

"I'll fight right by your side, brother."

Anghus gave a curt nod, and I turned to walk back to where Maison was talking to Ciaran. When I stood beside them, Maison held up a shirt.

"Lake's favorite shirt," he said. I took the shirt and brought it to my nose to get her scent. My dragon purred in my mind telling me that he had it and knew what we were looking for.

"Have you picked up anything?" I asked.

Maison nodded his head. "She was taken only just up the road. It was quick, and she had no idea it was coming. She didn't even have a chance to scream."

"Alright, let's go and follow the trail," I said as I stripped out of my shirt.

Ciaran's eyes were red and swollen from crying. "Find my girl, please."

I nodded my head and reached out my hand to squeeze his shoulder. "I will." It was a promise that I would keep. I would find her. I didn't know if I would see her alive, so I prayed to the creator that I would. But I would find her.

Maison and I stripped out of the rest of our clothes before calling forward our dragons. I could see Lake's aura as it wound around the house. Her aura was bright orange. In my shifted form, the scents were more potent, and Lake's smell was easier to pinpoint.

"Got it," Maison said through the link.

I nodded my head and lifted into the sky. Maison was close behind me. I glanced back down at the street. People milled about watching what was happening, a mixture of humans and supernaturals. AJE authority members moved up and down the road. I could easily pick out Lake's from all the auras I could see.

I floated through the sky, following the orange aura along the road. It was only a few hundred meters up the road when I saw where she was taken.

"There," I said, hovering over the top where Lake's aura got messy. I could see her panic; I could see that she was scared; her aura switched from the usual happy, bright orange to a flare of red with sparks flying from it.

"Demons," Maison said as he pointed his head toward where the black aura intermingled with Lake's.

"That would make sense," I replied. The black and orange auras appeared to be fighting, which would make sense with an abduction. I looked up the road where the black and orange aura continued. They were a tangled mess. Sometimes the black would cover the orange and twist around.

"She gave them a fucking good fight," Maison chuckled.

"She did. I just hope that she is still alive."

"I think she is. But for how long, I don't know."

I nodded and continued to fly through the sky, following the black and orange auras through the streets. I continued until we flew over the industrial area of Lalbert. It was all factories and abandoned buildings. A typical hiding spot for Ettore.

Finally, the black and orange aura stopped in front of a large warehouse. A huge sign was out the front that read, 'Synecology Research Center.' "It's another facility," Maison groaned.

"What does it mean?" I asked.

"Synecology is the study of animals."

"Shifters."

"Yep. What kind of supernatural is the girl?" Maison asked as he floated over the top of the facility.

"Pixcu."

"A rare shifter."

Nerves filled my belly. Lake was one of the only pixcus left alive in the world, and now Ettore had her. That thought was terrifying. As far as I was aware, there was only a handful of other pixcus living in the forbidden city in China.

"A cross between a tiger and a dragon. She shifts into a tiger with wings and horns. The horns are venomous," I explained.

"That would make sense as to why Ettore wants her. I bet he is going after the children born as rare supernaturals."

"What do we do? Do we go in?" I asked.

Maison shook his head. "No. Not alone. There are a lot of demons in there. Ettore is in there, and it is guarded heavily. We need backup."

"Alright, let's go back and let them all know."

Maison nodded his head before turning and flying back towards Memphis's home. In the distance, we could see Arcadia's dragon in the sky.

"Found her," I announced as we reached Arcadia.

"Yes. We are going to need to plan this one. It is far too dangerous to go in quickly."

I nodded my head. I just hoped that Lake would survive long enough for us to come up with a plan to rescue her.

Chapter Five

Flame

"What's your name?" I asked the girl as I sat watching her. I hadn't been able to leave. I knew Eric would probably be furious with me, but something about her kept me there. Maybe she hadn't been chosen to be here, like me. Or perhaps it was that she was so young, still a child.

The girl looked up at me with a sigh. "Lake. What's yours?"

"Flame. How old are you?"

"Fifteen," she replied before bringing her knees up to her chest and hugging them. "I'm scared."

I nodded my head. "That's understandable. Eric is an evil man."

Lake cocked her head to the side and frowned. "Eric?"

"Yeah, the one that captured you."

"You mean Ettore."

I shook my head. "You said that before; I heard someone else call him that too. But we were always taught his name was Eric."

"Do you know what he is doing?"

"You mean here?" Lake nodded her head. "He is breeding omegas. I don't know what he does with the babies."

Lake's frown pinched at her brow as she shook her head. "Flame, he is raising them to be a supernatural army. He wants to kill all humans and enslave the supernaturals. Once they are no longer good to him, he will kill them too. He wants to allow the demons to roam the earth and have free passage through the underworld and earthside. Then I believe he will try and take on middle earth to try and kill the gods and take their powers."

My eyes widened, and my mouth dropped open. I'd never heard of any of this. I didn't even know about gods or the underworld or middle earth. I shook my head. "Why does he want that? If he kills everyone, why bother taking the power of the gods?"

"He won't kill the demons, he will create new life by breeding the demons, and with the power of the gods, the demons will be too weak to rise up against him."

I scratched at my chin as I thought about what Lake was saying. Eric or Ettore was evil. He was narcissistic, and I wouldn't have put it past him to attempt something so crazy. It made sense to me.

"He asked me to kidnap a child," I blurted.

Lake cocked her head to the side. "Which child?"

"A valkyrie, her name is Hildr."

Lake's eyes widened. "He is planning on capturing all of the children prophesied about," she said with a gasp.

"What does that mean?"

Lake bit into her bottom lip before she shook her head. "I guess you haven't heard of the prophecy. Hel, the underworld goddess, got a message from the creator thousands of years ago that Ettore would one day create a supernatural war. Everything I told you about, the creator told Hel, and she wrote it down. But she also prophesied that children born with unique powers, unseen for thousands of years, would rise and fight against Ettore. He would lose to the children because they carried the power of the gods behind them. It is this new generation that it was prophesied about."

"How do you know?"

"Hel visited with different people. But Iver, the boy who will lead us, is also directly linked to the creator. He is the only cthulu on earth. The gods only create one cthulu when they are needed, and they are the ones that lead the rest of the supernaturals into battle. Iver is thirteen years old. It won't be long before he takes his place as the head of the army."

"But what if Ettore gets him? What if he is going to kidnap all the children?"

Lake's eyes welled with tears, and her chin wobbled with the weight of her emotions. "Then he will kill us, and we will lose the war."

I felt panic surge through my system. I had to do something to stop this. I didn't know what or how, but there had to be a way for me to protect the children so that they could have a chance at beating Ettore.

We were sitting in silence, weighing up all the information that had been shared, when suddenly screams echoed throughout the room. I gasped and stood quickly, pushing myself hard against the wall and using the shadows to hide me. The door to the chambers opened, and one of the alphas that worked with Ettore, Bjorn, stepped into the room carrying a screaming child over his shoulder. I watched wide-eyed as he opened a cell door and threw the child unceremoniously onto the floor. The child skidded across the floor before abruptly stopping at the wall.

I stared at the child who huddled against the wall. He lay still, and I wondered if he had been more injured than appeared. But as soon as Bjorn left the room, the boy uncurled and sat up.

"Lake," he gasped.

"Forrest," Lake replied with tears. "He is going after us all. And he wants the adults to come to kill them." I stepped out of the shadows. Forrest gasped, and Lake shook her head. "He is trapped here like us too. This is a breeding facility."

"I'm going to stop him," I announced. "I'll go and find whom I need to find and then tell them what Ettore is planning."

Lake nodded her head.

"He will kill you if he finds out," Forrest said quietly.

"Then I'll take that death if it means that I can help stop him."

I stood to leave. "Good luck, Flame. The gods are on your side," Lake called. I didn't look back as I left the cells and went in search of Ettore. It was time to end this. I wouldn't let him take anymore children. Not while I was still alive.

Chapter Six

Jericho

"The building is surrounded by other warehouses. The one to the right looks abandoned, but the one to the left looks like a panel beating place," I explained to everyone as we stood in Memphis's living room.

Lynx's phone started to trill, and he swore when he wrestled it out of his pocket. Something in his aura sent the entire room to silence.

"Colt, what's wrong?" Lynx answered.

Colt's panic sounded through the speaker. "It's Forrest; he took Forrest."

"Fuck," Lynx roared. "How was Forrest able to be taken?"

"I don't know. I turned my back for two minutes, and River came running through the front door screaming that someone had taken Forrest."

"He took him from the compound?" Anghus asked with apparent panic setting on his face.

"Yes," Colt replied. "The boys were out in the front garden. How did he get in?"

"I don't know." I knew that if we didn't get these kids back soon, Lynx would be on the warpath. "The wards were tightened. There should have been no way that he could get through," Lynx said. The look in his eyes was complete panic. His aura swirled around him with fury.

Ettore had just fucked with some dangerous people. The problem was that Ettore was just as dangerous and unhinged.

"We will get him back," Pax said quietly, but I could see the worry in his eyes. If Ettore had managed to get into the Devil's Advocates compound, there was no keeping the other children safe.

"Get all the kids and omegas to the AJE authority," Kade said. "I'm sending the witch and warlock team out to go with them as protection. I won't have any more children taken."

Memphis nodded his head, and Pax pulled his phone from his pocket, placing it to his ear as he walked out of the room. I scrubbed my hands up over my face. I was worried, not just for the children that had already been taken but also for my nephews and nieces. I didn't know what Ettore had planned for the children. I wasn't sure if they would even be alive once we could get in and save them.

Suddenly Anghus's phone started ringing shrilly. "Iver," he answered. "What can you tell me?"

I couldn't hear what Iver said, but Anghus looked up with wide eyes. "We can't go in. He has taken the kids to try and lure us to him. It's a trap."

"I am fucking going in. I'm not leaving my son in there," Lynx snapped.

Anghus nodded his head. "I know, I want to go in too, but if you get killed, then Forrest might get killed too. We don't know what Ettore is planning with the kids. For all we know, he will kill us and then immediately kill the kids."

Tears were in Lynx's eyes as he shook his head. "I can't do this, Anghus. I can't sit back and leave my son in the hands of that cunt."

Anghus reached out his hand and squeezed Lynx's shoulder. "I know that," he replied as he pressed his head into Lynx's forehead, looking down into his eyes. "We will get him out. I promise you. We need to do it smartly."

Lynx nodded, but he didn't look convinced. I knew Anghus would have to watch his vice president closely. The man was desperate to rescue his son. I glanced around the room and saw that everyone looked lost. Poor Ciaran hadn't stopped crying since we'd first arrived.

We needed to get in and save the kids. But how did we do it without leading lambs to slaughter? I lifted my thumb and chewed my nail as I wracked my brain with a way to do it.

"I'm enabling a team of supernaturals and humans to go in," Kade said.

"They will be killed," Anghus replied with a shake of his head.

"I don't think they will be," Kade replied. "Ettore wants the ones who are crucial to the war. He wants the ones who were involved in shutting down his facilities."

"How does he know who is responsible for that?" I questioned. "Won't he be blaming all of the AJE authority?"

Kade sighed and shrugged his shoulders. "I don't know. But we need to take the risk."

"What is the security like over there?" Bacchus asked, turning towards Arcadia and Maison.

"He has several alpha supernaturals. They are some of the alphas that he has trained. A mixture of demons and other species. The few you must be aware of is a mighty phoenix," Arcadia explained.

"As powerful as five?" Anghus questioned.

Arcadia smirked. "No phoenix is as powerful as Five."

"Do we get him to help us?" I asked.

Anghus hummed and glanced at Lynx. "You know what, I think he could work, and Ettore wouldn't be expecting him."

Arcadia nodded her head and glanced at Kade. "What do you think?"

Kade sighed, and his lips twisted to the side. "I've seen the powers of all the number children. Would you be against us asking them to help?" he asked, glancing at Anghus.

"Which ones are you thinking?"

"Five for sure. He is pretty much unkillable. But I'm also thinking Six."

Anghus winced. "You want her to seduce someone?"

"Ask Trudy before we ask Six; she is still learning her powers and is overcoming past trauma," Lynx said.

Kade nodded his head. "What about others?"

"The only other one that could be helpful without risking themselves is Seven," Lynx said.

"What can Seven do?" I asked.

"Control the weather."

I nodded my head. "That's actually a good idea. If seven creates an earthquake or storm, it draws out some of the security. Trudy can then work her magic. Me, Maison, and Arcadia can go in."

I looked over at Kade, who nodded his head. "I don't want the three of you going in on your own. Five will go in with you. But I'm also going to send in some vampire and mix teams."

"Mix team?" Anghus asked.

Kade nodded his head. "I've been working with another team; it is made up of a few different mystical supernaturals that we can use."

"Is there some that would be useful in this scenario?" I asked.

Kade nodded. "Yep. There are two other dragon shifters, an elf, and a demon."

My eyes widened. We had a demon working with the AJE authority?

"Alrick?" Pax asked.

Kade nodded his head and winked. "He just passed his exam."

"He will kill Alrick," Memphis gasped.

"He is strong. His power is much stronger than Ettore even can begin to realize," Raiden said.

I knew Alrick. I had only met him a few times when we had a catch-up at the Devil's Advocates compound, but I knew he was an omega. That didn't necessarily mean he was weak, but I was still worried.

"Trust me. I know what power he has. He will be able to shake things up," Kade said.

"Alright. Let's go get my boy," Lynx growled.

Kade smiled and nodded as he pulled his phone from his pocket and started to make calls.

Chapter Seven

Flame

I scurried up the stairs to the main facility floor. I needed to find the people that Lake and Forrest came from to warn them not to try and rescue them. There had to be a solution. I reached the main quarters where the alphas and Eric hung about. Ettore. His real name was Ettore, and he was creating a war. He wanted to enslave supernaturals. Ettore wanted the power of the gods. This just made him even worse in my eyes.

Ettore was sitting on a couch. His head was thrown back, and his eyes closed. At his feet, an omega kneeled, her head bobbing up and down on his cock. A shudder rolled over me at the sight. A chuckle fell from Ettore's lips, and when I glanced at him, I noticed him watching me.

"For all the times you've been fucked in the ass, you think a blow job wouldn't horrify you," he said as the girl continued slathering over his dick.

It was true that I'd been raped plenty of times. It was never pleasurable; I hated it and the men who fucked me. But I'd been raised to believe that it was the role of the omega to be fucked to be impregnated. However, in my case, it was never through fucking that I got pregnant. I was only ever given implants. It was like Ettore had a rule for me, no alpha was allowed to cum inside me.

Tears streamed down the girl's face. She wasn't one of the omegas I knew, but that didn't mean a lot. We, omegas, didn't get a chance to socialize. It was our role to serve Ettore.

"Come and sit down," Ettore said, pulling me out of my disgust.

I bit into my lip and sucked in a deep breath. If I wanted to beat him, I had to play his game. Forcing my body to move, I walked over to the couch and sat beside him, leaving a good gap between us. Ettore looked at the doorway where a few of the alphas stood watching, salivating, longing for their turn.

"Get a girl in here," Ettore instructed.

One of the men in the doorway nodded their head and turned. "I can't," I said quietly.

"You'll feel a lot better afterward."

My whole body was trembling. I wasn't sure I would be able to do this. I had so much on my mind, and I wasn't entirely sure I could even hide it all from him. I scrubbed my hand up over my face and closed my eyes. If only I'd had the chance to be successful in my escapes all those times. I didn't know how he had managed to find me, but every time, I was dragged back.

The alpha sent to fetch a girl came in with a naked omega on his arm. The girl couldn't have been much older than eighteen. Her eyes were wary, and she was heavily pregnant. From her scent, I could tell that she was fae.

"Well, get your dick out," Ettore growled, glancing over at me.

I hesitated before shaking my head. "I can't do this."

"You can and you will," Ettore growled. He may have said it with a smile, but there was a threat of violence hanging in the air.

Sucking in another deep breath, I quickly unzipped my jeans and slid them down my thighs. My cock hung flaccid against my balls. I wasn't interested in having my dick sucked. It wasn't that I didn't like a blow job. I'd never had one, but I'm sure I would like it. The thought of having my dick sucked by a girl that was given no choice was so unappealing; I was surprised my dick hadn't curled up inside me.

Ettore chuckled and shook his head. "Look at you, so soft."

The girl brought in stood timidly, watching us with wide eyes. Her body was shaking, and I could almost taste her fear. My cheeks flushed with embarrassment.

"What are you waiting for, girl? Get on your knees. You've been trained; you know what to do," Ettore snarled as he tangled his fingers into the hair of the girl who kneeled at his feet. He thrust his hips, and I felt my stomach roil as the girl choked and gagged around his shaft that was being stuffed into the back of her throat.

Ettore growled in pleasure. I breathed in deeply and slowly let it out. The girl, directed to suck my dick, kneeled at my feet and looked up at me through her lashes. Timidly she reached out a trembling hand and lifted my soft dick; moving forward, her tongue licked over the head, causing me to hiss.

I tried to think of everything I could to stop it from getting hard. But it didn't matter what I did; with the girl touching and sucking on my cock, it grew. The pleasure wrapped around me, and my disgust was soon forgotten as she slid her mouth up and down my shaft. She gently rolled my balls with one hand and scratched her nails over my taint. I held my body still so as not to thrust into her mouth.

Tears leaked from my eyes as I threw my head back. I was so conflicted. I wanted it all to stop, but at the same time, it felt so fucking good; I knew I wouldn't be able to hold back my orgasm.

Clawing at the armrest of the couch and my thigh, I felt my balls draw up. I could hear Ettore roar as he exploded in the girl's mouth. The scent of my arousal filled the air, and my toes curled. Opening my eyes, I took a chance to look down at the girl sucking my dick. Tears streaked down her cheeks and mixed with disgust and hatred when she looked at me. Nausea swept over me at the same time my cock exploded.

"Please stop," I grunted as soon as my cock dribbled the last bit of cum. The girl leaned back on her knees but kept her head down. A slight sniffle was all the sound she made.

My tears ran in a steady stream down my cheeks. I felt so much guilt, disgust, and remorse for my actions. I hated myself. I was no better than Ettore.

"Go and find the girl," Ettore said to me quietly. His voice was a low growl. "And Flame, you cross me, and I will fucking skin you alive."

Chapter Eight

J ericho

"Alright, everyone is here," Kade said as he entered the shifter room at the AJE authority. We knew we would have to plan this quickly; Lake and Forrest wouldn't have much time left. The longer this took, the more likely something horrible would happen to them. I couldn't stand the thought of it.

"We have the location; I've got a team of shadow walkers on the perimeter," Kade explained. He looked up at Anghus. "Israel is inside?"

Anghus nodded his head. "Yep, he made entry a few minutes ago. He has seen Ettore in the main room; he looks like he is getting impatient waiting for us."

Kade nodded. "I can imagine he is. He knows we would do anything to get those children back; the key is to do something he least expects."

Arcadia stepped forward. "I've been able to get a clearer picture," she said, looking over at Maison, leaning against one wall. "Correct me if you've got something different. But from what I can see, there are ten alphas plus Ettore. There are seven demons, all low ranking and not very powerful. Lake and Forrest are being held in an underground basement that he has converted into cells. They are warded, making it difficult to get them out."

"Shit," I spat as I thrust my hands up through my hair.

Maison nodded his head. "They are heavily warded, but I believe that either Kade or Scout could make it through them. The wards were created by Ettore."

Kade nodded his head and looked over at Scout. "I'll start working on them with Kaki," Scout said.

"Don't get seen," Arcadia warned.

Scout smiled and shook their head. "I'll shift and place a glamour over Kaki; if we keep her to the back of the abandoned building next door, we should be fine."

"If I can get into the abandoned building, I'll have more cover," Kaki said.

Scout nodded their head. "Let's go. I'll contact you when I've got more information."

"Okay," Kade replied as Scout and Kaki walked out of the room. "What else have you heard from Israel?"

"He's found the kids; they are safe, like Arcadia said, being held in a cell. There are plans to take the others, so it was good that we had them all moved here. Apparently, he is sending out his alphas."

"But it still doesn't tell us how someone was able to get in to grab Forrest," Pax said. He looked furious; I could tell his rhino was close to the front. His muscles were bulging, and he'd have torn out of his shirt with one wrong move.

"Yeah, I'm researching that. I've spoken to Vaughan, who was at the front gate; he said that we've had no visitors today," Anghus explained.

"You've had trouble with Vaughan before," I said, wondering if perhaps he was double-crossing the club.

Anghus shook his head. "We have, but I know it wasn't him."

"It wasn't," Maison said. "Ettore has a shadow walker alpha on his team."

I groaned, and Arcadia gasped. "I didn't know there were shadow walkers left on earth other than the ones we had here."

"There wasn't," Maison said. "But he had either bred one or has managed to kidnap one from the other side."

"Wait, excuse my ignorance," Alrick said. "But what is a shadow walker?"

"Basically, a ghost. They aren't real people. They are spirits of the dead. They are the ones that haven't crossed over because they feel they need to repay for what they did while they were alive," Maison explained.

"So, like a restless spirit?" Jai asked.

Maison nodded his head. "Anyone that dies is given a choice, to cross to the other side or to remain on earth as a shadow walker. The rule, however, is that as your role as a shadow walker, you can only do good deeds, or you risk being sent to purgatory."

"How could Ettore have bred one if they are dead?" I asked.

"Using necromancy. He would have to work closely with a blood witch who works in necromancy. Still, it is possible to create your own shadow walker by cutting off the doorway from someone to cross over," Arcadia explained.

"So, he killed someone or held onto their spirit here? Or he is just stealing a sole of some poor innocent fucker," Anghus growled.

Arcadia nodded her head. "I'm putting my money on that he killed someone."

"Why would they work for him, though?"

"They might feel like they have no choice. Ettore is a persuasive man; he can get what he wants easily. But he also uses threats. If he has threatened someone that they would never see their family again or be able to cross over, they might agree."

"They will eventually rot," Kade interjected.

"Rot?" Bacchus asked.

Kade nodded his head. "If a spirit is kept from crossing over using necromancy for a long time, they begin to rot. Their soul starts to die. As that happens, they go insane and usually become evil."

"Exactly what Ettore would want," I groaned.

"Yes."

"And the shadow walkers we have working for us? They aren't going to rot?" Memphis asked.

Kade shook his head. "No. They aren't because they are only here for a short time to do one last good deed before they cross over. All the shadow walkers that help us today will cross over probably tonight. As soon as their job is done. But they can't cross over if they are being held here through magic; it effectively shuts off the doorway for them."

"Jesus. This just gets worse and worse," Coltrane groaned from beside me.

"This is why we need to shut him down," I spat, my anger rising at the thought of what he was doing. Not just to the living but also to the dead.

"And we will," Arcadia growled.

Chapter Nine

Flame

Ettore's words rang in my brain as I ran from the building quickly. I had so many decisions running through my head. I could use this as an opportunity to escape. I could just forget about the kids and run for my life. Although I still didn't know how Ettore knew where I was every other time I'd escaped. But previously, I didn't have his permission to leave the facility; this time was different.

I could do what he wanted: find the valkyrie child and bring her back to Ettore, winning his favor. Or I could go and see the people that were going to rescue Lake and Forrest, warn them, and hopefully work with them to get myself safe.

I already knew that I couldn't take the child; there was no way that my conscience would allow it. I also didn't know the people that Lake and Forrest were worried about rescuing them. I jogged down the street away from the facility. I didn't know where I was, but it didn't matter. Ettore had firmly planted in my mind where I could find the child.

I had a choice to make, and I had to make it soon. Stopping on the side of the road, I scrubbed my hands up over my face. I looked up into the sky; above, two birds flew around and just above the facility while what appeared to be two dragons soared higher. I rubbed at my eyes wondering if I was seeing things.

I was still glaring into the sky when suddenly I felt myself being pulled into the shadows by hands I couldn't see.

"Stay quiet," a deep voice spoke from beside me.

I turned my head to try and find the owner of the voice, but there was nothing but a shadowy shape beside me.

"Who are you?" I whispered. My fear ramping up. Was this Ettore? Was this his plan, to pretend to let me be free only to pull me back?

"The question is, who are you? What were you doing in the facility?" the voice growled.

"I was born there."

The shadow beside me rippled, and suddenly I could make out a man's face. He didn't appear very old, with long curly hair and green eyes.

"Did you escape?"

I shook my head. "I was let free."

The man raised his brow and cocked his head to the side. I could tell he didn't believe me, but I didn't know if I could trust him with my information. I breathed in deeply as I weighed up my options.

"I was let free to do a job," I amended.

"What job?"

"I was supposed to kidnap a child. I wasn't going to be doing it. Still, I was trying to decide if I should run away or find the people that were going to rescue the children that had already been kidnapped," I blurted. Immediately I wondered if I was going to regret my decision.

The man stared at me for a little longer before he moved. I don't know how he did it, but I felt transported through time. Nausea swept over me, and I wasn't sure if I would pass out as my head spun with inertia. It was only a matter of seconds when I blinked my eyes again and saw that I was no longer standing near the facility but outside a house.

A large man with long brown hair and a glare that had me shaking in my shoes stepped towards me.

"What's your name?" he asked.

"Flame," I responded quietly.

The man nodded his head. "I'm Anghus. Kade will be here soon; we want to know what you know."

"Are you the ones that are going to rescue the two children?" I asked. Anghus gave a curt nod of his head. "It's a trap. Eric wants you to go there to rescue the children so that he can kill you all as well as the children."

"Eric?" Anghus asked cocking his head to the side.

I shook my head and thrust my hands up through my hair. "Sorry. His name is Ettore. He always told us that his name was Eric. But it was Lake who told me that his name is Ettore."

"You saw Lake?" a more petite man gasped from the house's front door. He came rushing down the path to stand in front of me.

I nodded my head. "Yes. Her and another boy Forrest."

The two men glanced at each other. A car pulled into the curb, and another tall man, this one a vampire, stepped out. But he wasn't any ordinary vampire; he was powerful. I could feel his power as he approached me.

"Flame?" he asked. I nodded my head. "My name is Kade Sinclair; I'm the head of the AJE authority. Can I ask you some questions?"

I breathed out a sigh of relief. "You're the man that I was supposed to come to find."

"Who wanted you to find me?"

"Lake. She told me to find the AJE authority and tell them not to go to the facility; it was a trap."

Kade nodded and glanced at the woman who had gotten out of the car beside me. She nodded to Kade. "He's telling the truth."

"Right, let's go inside and talk."

Chapter Ten

J ericho

I remained high in the sky. I knew that if Ettore looked, he'd see Maison and me circling the warehouse, but I didn't care. I felt he was waiting for us and that it was a trap. I believed Iver that Ettore was hoping we'd storm the place. It didn't shake off the anxious feeling that swirled in my belly at the thought of Ettore harming the children he'd managed to get a hold of. The others were safely at the AJE authority and guarded by witches and warlocks who had doubled down on the wards.

Obviously, it was going to be challenging to keep a shadow walker out, which is why the children weren't going to be left alone at any stage. It was the only thing we could do to keep them safe.

"I've just seen someone come out of the building," Maison said through the link.

"Yep, I've got him," Scout replied. I watched as Scout flew closer to the building; Nova from the Onyx Rebels was shifted into her owl and hovered just above the roof.

Suddenly the person that had run from the facility and started down the street stopped. They looked like they were trying to weigh up something in their mind. From this distance, I couldn't tell whether the person was an alpha or omega. Or even what gender they were. They glanced into the sky before a shadow walker reached out and pulled them back, cloaking them into the shadow.

"They are going to take him to Kade," Scout said.

"Who is he?" I asked.

"He said he was born in the facility, and Ettore had let him out to try and kidnap one of the children, but he wasn't going to do it."

"Do you believe him?" I asked.

"I don't know. I couldn't get close enough to read him, but Arcadia will meet him with Kade and be able to tell."

"At least all the kids are safe at the AJE authority," Nova said.

"Yeah, let's just hope that Lake and Forrest remain safe, too," I replied.

"They are still alive now. But I don't want to waste too much time, I think the longer they are in there without protection, the more desperate Ettore will get, and he isn't above killing one of the kids to prove a point," Scout growled.

My heart jolted in my chest at the thought of one of the kids being killed. There wasn't any good way to win this easily, and worry filled my soul with the idea of what this might cost us. We were stuck.

"Kade's got the guy. His name is Flame. He is fae, and he is telling the truth," Scout suddenly announced.

"Shit, is he safe now?" I asked.

"He will be. We will see to it. Let's head back to the house; the Devil's Advocates are there with the new crew to go in."

I turned in the sky and flew towards Memphis's house. All I could hope was that this would end with as little death on our side as possible. But I wasn't convinced it was going to happen. I was curious to meet Flame. Having him work for us was in our favor, and I wondered why he chose to turn his back on Ettore.

Ettore had to have trusted him if he had sent him. It wasn't like Ettore to be so remiss, he didn't make mistakes quickly, and this looked like it was a big mistake. I just hoped that if we put our trust in Flame, it wouldn't bite us in the ass later.

I landed in the front yard of Memphis and Ciaran's home. The street was still crowded with people, and I knew this must have been a strange sight to the humans. It wasn't that we hid. It was more that Dragons were private; we didn't like the attention that our alter brought to us. Dragons didn't tend to shift often in the open. So, when we did shift, we did it where no one saw; we would fly out over the ocean or high enough in the sky that we wouldn't be seen by the naked eye.

Not to mention that now, with Maison, Nova, and Scout standing beside me, there were four of us, all naked. Humans cared a lot more about their nudity than shifters did. We weren't bothered by it, mainly because it was just a normal part of being a shifter. But for humans, being naked in the street was taboo. Considering there were now four of us standing together on the front lawn, slowly dressing, one with no discernible genitalia, it was a sight to behold.

Bacchus came down the front step toward me as I slipped my shirt over my head. "What were you able to find out from Flame?" I asked.

"He's above board, it seems, but I'll get you, Scout, to check, just in case Arcadia missed something." Scout nodded their head and moved into the house. "He has been through hell. His entire body is carved with scars. He told us that he'd tried to escape many times in the past, but Ettore was always able to find him. However, he was chosen to abduct Hildr because the demon had failed during the fire, and Flame was in the wrong place at the wrong time. He doesn't think Ettore trusts him; he was threatened before leaving."

I sighed and shook my head. "Omega?"

Bacchus nodded. "Yeah. He's had two kids."

"How old?" Nova asked.

"He's twenty-one. His kids are still in the facility, but he doesn't know which one they are."

"How didn't you guys know about this facility?" Maison questioned.

"Ettore is using the name Eric Shutter for this one. Once again, he is selling it as a research center. We now have a team looking into all the research centers around Australia to ensure they aren't being run by Ettore under false names."

"How likely is it?" I asked. My head was spinning. I wasn't even inside this, yet I could feel just how far behind we were in stopping Ettore.

"Pretty likely. Just from a small google search, I think there are at least another seven, just here in Lalbert alone."

"Christ," Maison spat, shaking his head. "Whatever you need, count me in. This piece of shit needs to die."

Bacchus nodded. "And he will."

Chapter Eleven

Flame

"What can you tell us about the facility?" Kade asked.

I was sitting on a huge leather couch. I felt awkward having all these people staring at me, waiting for me to tell them everything.

"It is built on two levels. The first level is broken into living quarters for the omegas and children on one half, and then the other half is where the alphas live," I described. "Then, under the first level is a series of cells. That is where Lake and Forrest are being held. Those cells are warded heavily because Eric, I mean Ettore, uses them to put unruly omegas."

"How many omegas and children are in the facility?" Arcadia asked.

"There are four omegas, not including me. Two women and two men. There are twelve children, ranging from a newborn birthed yesterday to six. I believe that child might be one of mine, but I can't say for sure."

"What species are the children?" Memphis asked.

"Cambion," I replied.

Memphis frowned and shook his head before looking over at Arcadia. "Have you heard of cambion before?"

Arcadia nodded her head. "It's been a long time. But they are the byproduct of a fae and demon mating."

I nodded my head. "Most of the alphas are a demon. A couple isn't, but the majority are a demon."

"How many alphas?" Kade asked.

I hummed as I thought about how many of the alphas I'd seen in the building last. "I think there are about seven."

"And they are armed? Guards?"

"I don't think they carry weapons because they have powers. But their role is to guard the facility and breed with the omegas."

The door swung open and closed again, drawing my attention. I glanced up at the two men that walked into the living space. My eyes widened as the scent of melted chocolate surrounded me. One of the men stopped dead in the doorway and stared at me with wide eyes.

"Holy shit," he whispered.

"What?" the other man said, glancing at the first.

"He's my mate."

My mouth dropped open at the words. Mate? I'd heard about mating, but it was never in my cards. I was an omega from a breeding facility. I was never going to have the opportunity to find my mate. Yet I sat there staring at a beautiful man with cropped dark hair and muscles that rippled beneath his tight shirt.

"Fuck, we don't have time for that," Memphis growled, drawing my attention back to him. I shook my head and scrubbed my hand over my face.

"Are you going to go into heat?" Coltrane asked.

I shook my head. "No. I was given a heat suppressant when I accepted the job from Ettore."

Coltrane nodded. "Good, we can keep going then, and you can decide later if you want to mate with Jericho or not."

I cocked my head to the side as Jericho let out a low growl. He was glaring with narrowed eyes at Coltrane, who chuckled.

"Enough. No one wants your mate, Jericho," Kade growled. The tone of his alpha rippled through the air, and I watched Jericho physically deflate under the power.

"Sorry," he said, scrubbing his face with his hands.

"Alright, Israel is still inside the facility; he is in the cells with Lake and Forrest and will alert us if anything happens to them. If Ettore comes to get them, we will go in regardless of the danger to ourselves," Kade explained. "But first, I think we should send in the shadow walkers, followed by Five, Trudy, Kaki, and Scout. The shadow walkers will protect the kids along with Israel, should Ettore try to get to them. Once the alphas are disabled, Alrick will enter to break down the wards along with Kaki and Scout. Then the rest of the Shifter Unit, Onyx Rebels and Devil's Advocates, will go in to rescue the kids. Our biggest issue will be Ettore. He won't go down without a fight, and I suspect he will attempt to flee. That is a bridge we will have to cross later. Is everyone clear?"

I nodded, not that I was involved in the decision or the raid. A round of affirmations sounded through the room, and I watched as the various men and women turned to leave the house.

"Where do I go?" I asked quietly before everyone left.

"Arcadia, can you please take Flame back to the precinct where he will be safe," Kade asked.

Arcadia smiled and nodded her head. "Come on, let's go; the sooner we get out of here, the better." She reached out her hand, and suddenly we blinked out of the home we'd been in and flashed back into a large building filled with all sorts of different people. I stumbled slightly as a wave of dizziness washed over me.

"Sorry about that; it takes a little bit to get used to," Arcadia chuckled. "This is the AJE authority precinct; let's get you into a warded room. I'm sorry that there won't be much to do except watch television, but we will rustle you up some food, and you will be safe."

I smiled at Arcadia. "Thank you."

I hoped that this would be the start of a potential new life. One that was free of Ettore, but the fear was still in my mind. He could come and take me at any stage. And I truly believed that he would skin me alive when he caught me. I just didn't know when or how.

Chapter Twelve

Fucking hell, my mate. I didn't even know what to think about it. I wasn't ever one that cared if I never met my mate. Unlike Obsidian, it just wasn't something I was interested in. But to see my mate standing there, my dragon was going crazy. He wanted Flame in every sense of the word. But it wasn't the right time. We needed to focus on the facility and the children that had been abducted.

We were getting ready to move in. Kade, Anghus, the Shifter Unit, and Onyx Rebels were on the edge of the industrial park. The shadow walkers had surrounded the facility and reported that no one had gone in or out since Flame had left. Maison and I circled high in the sky; we were both ready to grab anyone that escaped.

I wasn't sure if Ettore had cameras anywhere and could see us. We couldn't tell if he knew what we were planning. All I could do was hope for the best.

"Shadow walkers are in," Kade announced through the link. "Five, Trudy and Alrick enter now. Kaki, Scout, and I are right behind you."

"Going in," Alrick replied just as I watched him step out of the shadows, and the door disintegrated to nothing but rubble. Five stepped over the rubble of the door and entered the building, where shouts could be heard, and small explosions rocketed the building.

"Shit, that kid is powerful," Maison said quietly through the link.

I nodded my head as I watched for people running from the building. So far, so good. It seemed that Five, Trudy, Alrick, Scout, Kaki, Kade, and the shadow walkers were keeping it contained. I could hear different people shouting and swearing, but without being able to see, I didn't know what was happening.

"Onyx Rebels, Devil's Advocates, and Shifter Unit, enter now," Kade called.

People stormed towards the facility. I continued to hold my space in the sky, waiting to see if Ettore would escape. I didn't expect it, but I still hoped. I wanted nothing more than to kill him with a fatal blow.

"I'm down," Trudy cried.

"I've got her," Alrick replied.

After a few moments, Alrick appeared outside the building with Trudy in his arms. Even from this distance, I could see that she was pale and not moving. Flying down, I landed quickly in front of Alrick.

"What happened?" I asked through the link that Kade and Scout had opened for us to be able to communicate.

"She was stabbed," Alrick said. "I can heal her; I just need to be somewhere that we are safe."

I nodded and reached out to hold Alrick and Trudy in my talons as I lifted into the sky. Flying, I brought them to the abandoned building next to the facility.

Alrick leaned over Trudy, placing his hands on her stomach, where blood oozed from an open wound. I observed, keeping my eyes open to any danger that might come our way. Trudy groaned, and I turned to focus on her.

"Where are you, Jericho?" Kade called through the link.

"On the roof of the abandoned building next door. Trudy was stabbed; Alrick is healing her now."

"I'm coming now," Scout said.

I watched as Scout's raven flew up from the building next door and landed on the roof beside me. They altered and went to Trudy.

"The wound is healed," Alrick said.

Scout nodded their head, and they stroked a hand over Trudy's hair. The siren blinked her eyes open and smiled gently.

"How are you feeling?" Scout asked.

"Like I got stabbed," Trudy laughed. "But I'm okay. Thank you for healing me, Alrick."

Alrick smiled and nodded his head. "Anytime."

I drew my dragon back and walked over to Scout, Alrick, and Trudy. "Did you get Ettore?"

Scout shook their head. "He did what I had assumed he would do and blinked out of the place and back to the underworld."

"Damn it," I swore.

Scout shrugged their shoulders. "We will get him when the time is right."

"Are the kids safe?" Trudy asked.

Scout nodded. "Yeah, very shaken up but safe. We've arrested all the alphas and rescued the omegas and children."

"Good. That's one less facility he has access to," I said just as flames started to lick at the old facility. I watched it burn; never been so happy to see a burning building in my life.

Maison flew down and landed beside me before altering. "I've let Marlan know. He is sending trucks are coming to put the fire out, but not too quickly. We need to let it burn down a bit so that it can't be repaired easily."

"Good," I replied with a sigh. My mind turned back to Flame. My mate. I worried that Ettore might attempt to get to him, especially now that we'd destroyed the facility. Worry bubbled in my stomach as I thought about what could happen.

Chapter Thirteen

Flame

"It's going to be alright," the boy named Iver said as he sat beside me. I sighed and glanced over at him. I'd met all the kids that were talked about in the war prophecy. They were amazing. And there was so much power in the room I couldn't quite get over it.

"I hope so," I replied. "I'm just worried that Ettore will hunt me down."

Iver nodded his head. "Do you know that you have a tracker in your body?"

My eyes widened, and I shook my head. "No. Is that how Ettore can always find me?"

Iver nodded his head before turning to the lady named Merza.

"Merza?" he called. Merza turned and wandered over to where we sat. "Flame has a tracker in his arm. Can we get it out of him to stop Ettore from knowing where he is?"

Merza's eyes widened. "Oh my, yes, of course. Do all the people from the facility have trackers?"

I shrugged my shoulders. "I don't know. I didn't even know I had one in me."

"They do. I don't know what it is about this facility, but it's the only one that we've shut down so far that Ettore has put trackers in," Iver said.

Merza hummed. "Okay, let me organize some things, and we can take it out. Iver, do you know exactly where the tracker is?"

Iver nodded his head and reached out his hand to my wrist. He ran his fingers over a spot just above my wrist joint. Merza nodded and pulled a pen from her pocket, quickly circling where Iver pointed.

"Alright, I'll get organized, and we will get it out of you. Ettore can't get in here, so you are safe, but I want to get it out of you before you leave."

"Where will I go?" I asked.

Merza hummed. "That's a good question."

"I'd like to hope he'd come home with me," a deep voice said behind me.

I spun in my seat to see Jericho standing there. He was watching me with a slight smile on his lips. My eyes widened, and my belly fluttered with excitement.

Merza chuckled. "I see we have a future-mated couple."

Jericho smiled and nodded his head. "Of course, that is if Flame wants me."

I stood; my body was in control as it moved on autopilot toward Jericho. "I want you."

Jericho reached out and skimmed his fingers down my cheek.

"I don't mean to interrupt, but the fact that you are here means that the raid was successful?" Merza asked.

Jericho glanced up and nodded his head. "Yes. All the alphas were arrested, and the omegas and children were rescued. Unfortunately, we couldn't capture Ettore."

I felt disappointment hit me in the guts at the thought of Ettore escaping.

Merza sighed and shrugged her shoulders. "That was to be expected. Did everything go smoothly?"

"No, not completely. Trudy was stabbed. However, Alrick and Scout healed her, so she is okay now."

I winced. "I'm sorry," I said quietly.

Jericho looked down at me. "Why are you sorry?"

"I kind of feel responsible. Maybe it wouldn't have happened if I'd given you more information or gone with you."

"I don't think so, Flame. It is a risk that all of us take every day. We are in a war against Ettore and those in his army, so it is to be expected," Merza said.

I sighed. I understood her words, and I even believed them. Still, because I had been living in the facility and saw Ettore regularly, I felt like I was somehow responsible for how things played out.

"I guess so. You got all the children out?" I asked, turning back to Jericho.

He smiled and nodded his head. "You have two children already?"

I nodded. "I think I know which children are mine, but I can't be certain because they are taken from us immediately, so we don't get to see what they look like or even know their gender. But I recognized their scent."

"We will do DNA tests to confirm," Merza said.

"I don't know what a DNA test is."

"All parents share biology with their children; DNA is that biology. We will test all the children with the omegas, and we will be able to tell which child belongs to which omega."

"Your children are Keleli and Sarlith," Iver said.

I smiled and nodded my head. One thing I'd learned since meeting Iver, he knew something that was out of this world.

"They are the two I'd thought," I answered.

Iver smiled. "That is the two we will DNA test first, then," Merza promised.

"Thank you."

"You don't have to thank me for that. But before you go anywhere with Jericho, let's first organize for someone to remove the tracker."

"Wait, what?" Jericho asked with astonishment.

Merza nodded her head. "This facility obviously means much more than we realized to Ettore, as all omegas and children have trackers."

"Shit. Have any of the others had it before?"

Merza shook her head. "Not that we've discovered."

"This one has trackers because all of the omegas are Ettore's children," Iver explained.

My eyes widened, and I gasped. "Really?"

Iver nodded his head. "Oh my. This turns some things on its head. I'm sorry, Jericho, but we might need to keep Flame here for a little longer until we can sort some things out."

Jericho nodded his head. "That's fine, but I'm not leaving him."

Merza smiled. "I didn't expect any less."

Chapter Fourteen

Jericho

I wasn't going to be leaving Flame's side. My dragon wouldn't let me, but I also didn't want to.

"I have a room available for you both if you would like some alone time," Merza said with a small smile. I glanced at Flame, whose cheeks blushed, but he nodded his head. "Alright, let's go. It's nothing flash, but it will give you a chance to get to know one another."

"Thank you, Merza," I said as we began to follow her through the AJE authority to a set of stairs below the main building.

"These are warded cells; it's the strongest part of the precinct, so you will be safe here," Merza said as we reached a large glass door. She pushed it open, and we walked into a long corridor with cells off each side. Some of the cells were filled with alphas who sat glaring at us.

Flame gasped as he looked into the cells. "These are the alphas from the facility," he said quietly.

One of the alphas stood and walked towards the door. Flame flinched, and I felt my dragon begin to pace, ready to protect my mate.

"Ettore will kill you for this," the alpha growled.

Merza chuckled. "Your threats mean nothing. You will be better off when you realize that you are just a pawn in Ettore's little power play."

The alpha blinked, and his head jerked back as if he hadn't realized that Ettore was just using him.

"He will come for me," he growled but didn't sound as confident as he had been. Merza chuckled before sighing.

"It's sad how brainwashed he has them. If they realized that Ettore couldn't care less about any of these people, they would be better off. The only one Ettore cares about is himself."

I nodded my head. It was true. So many people were utterly lost in this. Ettore didn't care. He didn't give a shit about the people and whom he stood on. He had his own agenda and would use anyone and everyone to get ahead.

The alpha remained quiet, but I could see his mind starting to tick over with Merza's words. She moved along the cells to the very end before opening a large steel door. All the other cells were cages, but this one had a solid door.

"Here you go, guys; I'm sorry it's not very romantic. But it will at least give you a bit of privacy and keep you safe," she said with a smile.

"Thank you, Merza," I replied as I stepped into the room.

Merza smiled and wiggled her fingers before she left the room, shutting the door behind her.

"Well, this is different," I said with a chuckle. "I didn't expect to meet my mate today."

Flame laughed and shook his head. "I didn't think I would ever meet a mate, so it's blown my mind."

I grinned and moved to sit on the bed, leaning my back against the wall. "Tell me about you?"

Flame shrugged his shoulders and moved to sit beside me. "I don't know what there is to tell. I'm twenty-one years old and a fae. I have two kids I didn't know until Iver said their names and I grew up in a facility."

"How come you weren't bred as often as other omegas I've heard of?"

Flame shrugged again and sat on the bed beside me, leaning his back against the wall. "I don't know. Other omegas in the facility were bred more often than I was. But I was only implanted twice."

"Wait? You didn't have sex to get pregnant?"

He shook his head. "No. That was the other difference. I was the only one that was ever implanted." Flame scrubbed his hands up over his face. "I feel like I've learned so much in just a short time. I mean to find out Ettore is my father. What the hell do I do with that?"

I reached out and clasped Flame's hand. "It is a shock, that's for sure. But it does mean one thing; you are more powerful than a normal Fae."

Flame sighed and nodded. "I guess you're right, but I don't know much about my power."

"You can learn. It will take time, but you will be able to learn."

Flame's eyes widened as if something had just occurred to him. "Holy shit," he swore.

"What?"

Flame shook his head. "If all the omegas at the facility belong to Ettore, something horrible happened to me this morning."

I frowned and shook my head. I didn't understand what he meant. "What happened?"

"I think I got a blow job from my sister."

My eyes widened, and I gasped. "What the fuck?" My dragon was going insane with jealousy, but I was horrified about the whole sister part.

"Before I left the facility to come and find you all," Flame groaned as he scrubbed his hands over his face. "Oh god. That is so fucking gross. Ettore was the one that demanded it happen. Fuck I think I'm going to vomit."

Flame leaped from the bed and fell to his knees in front of the toilet, heaving. Tears streaked down his cheeks. My heart ached for him, but my head was spinning. What the fuck was going on?

Chapter Fifteen

F lame

Oh god, almighty, I felt so ill. Ettore knew it. That evil bastard knew exactly what he was doing when he did it. Tears leaked over my cheeks as I purged everything in my stomach into the toilet. Jericho sat on the floor beside me, rubbing his hand up over my back. What a way to start mateship. I wouldn't be surprised if he didn't want me after this. My fucking sister.

A sob fell from my lips as my body shuddered under the weight of my disgust. I can't believe he did this. That's not true; I shouldn't be surprised at all. Ettore was a sick prick who didn't care about the aftermath of anything he did.

"I'm sorry," I cried to Jericho. "You must think I'm so disgusting."

Jericho chuckled and shook his head, skimming his hand up and down my back. "Not at all. I think you were tricked by an absolute piece of shit."

I sighed and leaned back on my knees, wiping my mouth with my sleeve. "I feel sick over this."

"I can tell. Who was the father of the children that were not implanted?"

I sighed and shrugged my shoulders. "Honestly, I don't know. I always assumed it was the alphas. But to be completely honest, I don't know anything anymore."

"It's alright. Look, you are safe now. You don't have to worry about Ettore anymore."

It wasn't true. It was a nice thought, but it just wasn't true. "Maybe when I remove the tracker, I will feel more confident. But I keep expecting him to just pop up at any moment like he did all the times I'd escaped."

Jericho looked at me, confused. "How did you escape other times?"

"I'd found ways to get out. I'd escaped probably around about fifteen times. Sometimes I would only get as far as the front gate, and other times I made it to the other side of Lalbert. But Ettore would always just pop out of the atmosphere in front of me and drag me back. I never knew how he did it, but Iver said I have a tracker on my wrist."

Jericho nodded his head. "What would happen to you when he caught you."

I skimmed my fingers over the large scar etched into my face. "This was the last time I escaped. The scars on my back, legs, and chest are from other times."

"He cut you?"

I nodded my head. "This one he did. But the ones on my back and chest were from beatings with whips."

Jericho growled and shook his head. "Fuck I hate him."

"Me too," I replied.

Jericho stroked his fingers down my cheek. "Do you realize how beautiful you are?"

I snorted. "That was a rapid change of subject."

Jericho blinked and shook his head. "Sorry," he replied with a slight blush, making me giggle again.

"Don't be sorry. I like it. Tell me about you?"

"Well, I'm twenty-six, and I'm a firefighter. I'm a dragon shifter."

"Was it you that I saw flying above the facility when I first left?"

Jericho nodded his head. "Yeah, me and Maison. He is one of my co-workers; he's a firefighter too."

"Your dragons were majestic."

"Thank you. My dragon is the iridescent blue one, while Maison is red."

I smiled and reached my hand out to touch Jericho's. "Do you want me to be your mate?"

Jericho's eyes flared, and his pupils blew wide. He swallowed thickly as he licked over his bottom lip. I watched the movement, wondering what his lips would feel like on mine. I quickly glanced around the room and noticed the toothbrush and toothpaste. Before we did anything, I quickly stood and went to the basin. Jericho watched me with amusement as I brushed my teeth.

Once I felt like I was clean again, I walked over to the bed and sat down, slipping my shirt off over my head and throwing it on the ground. Jericho watched me with lust all over his face. My cock was hard, and I could feel slick starting to drip from me. Jericho slowly stood and stalked over to where I sat.

"Can I kiss you now?" he asked.

I smiled and nodded my head. Jericho didn't wait; he moved forward and pressed his lips to mine. It was everything I had expected. His lips were soft, and the stubble on his chin grazed against my skin. I groaned as Jericho's tongue swept between my lips and tangled with mine.

Chapter Sixteen

J eričho

I thrust my hands into Flame's hair and tilted my head to deepen the kiss. Flame groaned against my mouth. The scent of his arousal filled the air around us. My cock was stiff and throbbing. My dragon was crowing with happiness about the decision to make Flame ours.

I would never end the kiss if I didn't have to breathe. I pressed my forehead against Flames.

"Do you want to be my mate?" I asked.

Flame nodded his head and bit into his pouty bottom lip. "Yes," he whispered.

I smiled and gently caressed my fingers down his chest, flicking my thumb over his peaked nipples. Flame's eyes rolled in his head, and he groaned. So sensitive. Guiding my hands down over his stomach and to the waistband of his jeans, I quickly worked the button and zipper. Flame lifted his hips to help me to ease his jeans off with his underwear. I tossed them to the side with his shirt and shoes.

I looked down over Flame's body. He was gorgeous. His skin was dotted with scars. I couldn't think about it. I wanted to skin Ettore for what he'd done to my mate. I stroked my fingers over his thighs to where his cock sat hard, weeping with precum.

My mouth watered with desire with the chance to taste him. I wanted to do everything. There wasn't going to be an inch on his body that I won't have licked by the time we were done. Flame was watching me as I took him in. He was tall and muscular, with blonde hair and green eyes that sparkled with lust.

"I want to see you," Flame whispered.

I stood from the bed and quickly ripped my shirt over my head. Kicking my shoes off with my toe, I unzipped my jeans and allowed them to fall from my hips and down my legs. I moved my hands to the waistband of my underwear and pushed them down.

Flame groaned as my cock bobbed from the confines of my boxers and jutted straight out. I stroked my hand over my shaft, delighting that Flame's eyes grew darker and his desire poured from him.

"Do you want this, Flame?" I asked.

Flame bit into his bottom lip as he looked up at me and nodded his head. "Yes."

I walked over to the bed and pressed my lips again to Flame's. He moaned and laid back on the bed. I followed him down and hovered over him with my elbows resting on either side of his head.

"I want you," Flame whispered breathlessly. I could feel his desperation. It was like his spirit was calling to mine. I moved my hips so that I skimmed the head of my cock up and down through the crease of his ass.

Flame hissed, and his eyes rolled. My cock was soaked in his slick, and with each pass over his asshole, I felt him tremble. Slowly I pushed inside him. Flame groaned, and he widened his legs. His fingers clutched at my shoulders as I went deeper inside the wet warmth of Flame's ass.

The minute I bottomed out, I watched Flame's face. His lips were popped open, and his eyes were rolled. I moved my hips experimentally. Flame cried out, and his nails tore at the skin on my back. The pinch of pain heightened my pleasure. I thrust my hips slowly. Flame continued to moan with every thrust. Every time my cock rolled over his prostate, his body tightened, and I knew he wouldn't be far away from his impending orgasm.

Reaching between our bodies coated with sweat, I circled my palm around Flame's cock and stroked the shaft.

"Oh god, yes, right there," he gasped as his ankles locked around my back.

I kept the pace of my hips and hand simultaneously as I felt the tingles spread from my cock to the base of my spine. My dick started to swell, and I knew my knot wouldn't be far off. My dragon was roaring in my head, demanding that we make Flame our own.

"Final chance to stop the mating," I warned.

"Bite me, damn it," Flame demanded with a cry.

It was all the permission I needed. My incisors lengthened, and I bit into the sensitive skin of Flame's chest. Flame's cry echoed around the room as I felt his cock jerk and cum coated my hand and stomach. My knot locked in place, and the moment I tasted Flame's blood on my tongue, my orgasm washed over me. However, nothing prepared me for that return mark. Flame's teeth penetrated my chest and sent me hurtling through the stratosphere. I filled Flame's channel with my seed over and over. I thought I would pass out from the pleasure. I'd never felt anything like it before.

Slowly I returned to reality and glanced down at my mate. Flame wore a serene smile on his lips as he opened his eyes to look up at me.

"We are mated," he said with awe.

I nodded my head and smiled. "We sure are, baby, we sure are."

"I like it."

"Me too."

Chapter Seventeen

Flame

I laid with my head against Jericho's chest. My mate. I would have laughed if someone had told me this would happen to me a week ago. I couldn't believe my fate. Jericho skimmed his fingers up and down my naked spine.

"What's your favorite color?" he asked.

"Red. Yours?" we had been playing fifty questions for the last half hour or so. The questions were interspersed with a quick hand job or blow job.

"Blue."

A knock sounded on the door. "Sorry to interrupt, boys," Merza's voice rang through the heavy steel door.

Jericho pulled the blanket up over our naked bodies. "It's okay," he called out.

"I've got the medic here to remove the tracker from Flame's arm when you are ready, but she can only be here for another hour or two."

"No worries, we will get dressed and come upstairs," Jericho said.

"Alright, I'll get it all sorted for you."

As Merza walked away, Jericho flicked the blankets from our bodies, and I climbed out of bed. My muscles ached, and a low throb in my ass made me smile. I skimmed my hand down over my belly.

"Do you think I might be pregnant?"

Jericho's eyes widened, and he gasped. "Oh my god, we could be fathers."

I giggled at his reaction and nodded my head. "Well, technically, I'm already a father."

Jericho hummed. "That's true. Do you know what you want to do about that yet? Did you want to take custody of the children?"

"Wait, you mean I can?"

Jericho smiled and nodded his head. "Yes. It will be your decision as to what you want."

I nodded my head. It wasn't something I'd ever given a thought to. In the facility, I didn't even know which of the children were mine. We were always told that the children wouldn't stay with us. Any alpha children would be raised to eventually join Ettore's army. The omega children went to be bred.

It made me wonder who the other biological father was of my children. I'd always assumed it was Ettore, but considering he was my father, that didn't make much sense. I wondered if there was a way to be able to tell.

"Ready?" Jericho asked once we were both dressed again.

"Definitely. I'll be glad to get rid of this," I said as I touched my wrist. I couldn't feel a tracker inside me, but I believed Iver that there was one there.

Jericho opened the door and guided me out into the hallway. The cells were still filled with the alphas from the facility. They sat or stood by the doors, glaring at me as I passed them. The one that had threatened me earlier sneered as we got closer.

"He won't let you get away with this, you know," the alpha growled.

I sighed and stood in front of the bars. "Do you really think he cared about any of us?"

The alpha looked up at me, and I could see the doubt in his eyes. He'd been brainwashed to believe that Ettore was the god he would follow blindly. He had wrongly thought that Ettore cared about him. Sadly, Ettore only cared about himself.

"He is going to come and get us," the alpha argued, but I could see he didn't honestly believe it.

I shook my head. "No, he won't. He will leave you here to rot. That facility wasn't the first that they shut down. It won't be the last. He doesn't care about any of you."

"It's true," Jericho said. "The alphas that the AJE authority has already arrested weren't saved. They are sitting in supernatural prisons. You'll see. The same place that you are going to end up."

The alpha blinked, and I could see his mind working overtime. I could tell that he didn't want to believe what we were saying, but at the same time, he was nervous that we were right.

"Good luck with the rest of your life, but if I was you, I'd give up this foolish idea that Ettore is going to save you," I said before I moved away from the cell and continued along the hallway.

The sooner the alphas began to see that Ettore was only in this whole thing for himself, the better.

Chapter Eighteen

Jericho

Merza was waiting with Kaylee, a medic that often worked alongside us and the AJE authority in a medical bay.

"Hey, Jericho. Congratulations," Kaylee said with a grin.

"Thank you. This is my mate, Flame." I smiled and wrapped my arms around the unicorn, kissing her on the top of the head.

"It's lovely to meet you, Flame. My name is Kaylee. I'm a medic and going to be taking out that tracker."

Flame smiled and nodded his head. "How will you know exactly where it is?"

Kaylee pointed towards an ultrasound machine that she had sitting on the bed. "This will show me where in your body it is. Have you ever had an ultrasound before?"

Flame shook his head. I could see the nerves that he was feeling. "Not even when you were pregnant?" Merza asked.

Flame glanced over at Merza with a slight frown on his face. "No. Once it was confirmed we were pregnant, we were put into the pregnancy quarters and left there."

Merza hummed but nodded her head. "Well, the ultrasound machine won't hurt you. But it will be able to pinpoint exactly where the tracker is so that Kaylee can get it out without too much pain."

"How will you get it out?" Flame asked.

"I'm going to numb the area with an injection. I warn you, the numbing stuff does sting. But once it takes effect, you won't be able to feel anything. I'll then make a small cut above where the tracker is and pull it out. You probably won't even need a stitch," Kaylee explained.

Flame nodded his head and bit into his bottom lip. "And all of the omegas and children had trackers?" he asked Merza.

Merza sighed and nodded her head. "Yeah. We've been able to remove them all. We can't get to the alphas as easily, but you're the last one left to have it removed."

Flame nodded his head and glanced over at me. "Will you hold my hand?"

"Of course, baby," I said, stepping towards my mate and taking his hand in mine.

"Okay, let's get you up on the bed and get started," Kaylee directed.

It only took a matter of moments before she had the tracker out and destroyed. Like she had said, Flame didn't even need a stitch. She placed a bandage over the wound and smiled down at Flame.

"You're good to go."

"Thank you," Flame said. "So, now Ettore won't be able to find me as easily."

Merza nodded her head. "That's right, but just to make sure, we have gone to Jericho's home and placed stronger wards around it. We assumed that was probably where you would be living."

Merza looked up at me, and I nodded my head. "As long as Flame would like to live with me, then yes, that's where we will live."

"I want to live with Jericho. What will happen to the children?"

"Well, for now, they are all still here, along with the other children of the Onyx Rebels, Devil's Advocates, and Shifter Unit. But as soon as the DNA test results return, we can know exactly which children belong to you. You will be given a choice: either take custody of them or, if you'd rather, they can live with the Devil's Advocates, Onyx Rebels, or we can find a family to adopt them."

Flame shook his head before looking up at me. "If it is alright with you, I'd like to take custody of my children."

I leaned forward and kissed the side of Flame's head. "Of course, that's alright with me. Why don't we go and spend some time with them."

Taking his hand, I led Flame from the medical bay and down to the large conference room where the children and their parents were currently staying. The room was filled with chatter and laughter. I glanced around and noticed that the children we'd rescued from the facility were all happily playing. At first glance, you wouldn't have even realized that these children had been living in a facility only a matter of hours earlier. Flame smiled and nodded his head.

"Hey there, you two," Bacchus said with a grin as he approached us.

"Hey. Bacchus, my big brother, and you already know Flame, my mate."

Bacchus nodded his head and opened his arms. "Welcome to the Rigby family. Wait until Mama hears that the last of her babies has found his mate."

I chuckled at the thought. Mama would be so excited. Just like she was for my brothers when they found their mates.

Chapter Nineteen

Flame

I was coming to terms with what it meant to have freedom. It was such a strange feeling. It didn't stop me from looking over my shoulder constantly. I kept expecting Ettore to pop up in front of me and whisk me away. But so far, I haven't seen him. Jericho always talked with his brother Bacchus, and the AJE authority said no one had seen him. Not even in the underworld.

Everyone I met on the outside had been fantastic. Jericho took me to the Devil's Advocates compound, where I spent time with my children. Well, who I thought was my children. Until the DNA tests came back, I wouldn't know for sure. They were living at the compound and seemed so happy. They were being taught in school how to read and write and were learning to use their powers. The best part was that they would learn to use their powers for good rather than whatever nefarious things Ettore had planned.

It had been two weeks since the rescue. I was feeling a bit antsy, I wanted to move forward, but until the DNA results came back, it wasn't possible. I was yet to find out if I was pregnant. I felt I was, but I'd yet to take a test to make it official. However, that was all going to change today.

I was standing in the bathroom with Jericho by my side as we stared down at the pregnancy test, waiting for it to tell us if I was pregnant or not.

"This feels like it's taking forever," I groaned.

Jericho glanced at his phone, where he had a timer running. "We've got another thirty seconds."

I groaned. How did two minutes seem to take an eternity? Finally, I saw the screen light up with a word, and my eyes widened. I let out a gasp and clutched at Jericho's arm. Pregnant. It said I was pregnant.

Jericho threw his head back and let out a long roar before turning to me and crushing me to his chest.

"We are going to be fathers," he cheered as he bounced up and down, making me laugh excitedly.

This was going to be the first pregnancy that I was genuinely excited about. I hadn't been excited through my last two pregnancies. A bubble of guilt grew in my belly. Ultimately, I knew I couldn't keep those babies, so I'd pushed any thoughts of care, love, and excitement away.

It was different now. Now I was going to have the chance to keep my baby. This baby would be raised by a loving family. Their Papa and Dad would protect them and show them what it was like to live in freedom. I hoped the DNA test would indicate that the children I'd had before were whom I thought they were. It would be wonderful to live as a family.

"I can't wait to tell Mama," Jericho laughed.

I'd learned much about Jericho's family over the last couple of weeks. He came from one of seven. Being the youngest, he said he'd always been spoiled. I couldn't wait to meet his Mama, Papa, and other brothers. Jericho was the last to be mated, but that didn't remove any of the excitement his Mama had gushed over the phone when Jericho called her.

"I bet she will be so happy," I said with a grin.

Jericho chuckled and nodded his head. "No matter how many kids we have, she will be equally excited for them. She adores all her grandbabies."

I smiled. "I like that. I can't wait to meet your family." So far, I'd only had the opportunity to meet Bacchus and Obsidian. But if they were all like them, then I knew I would love all of his brothers.

Jericho nodded his head. "We will be catching up with them on the weekend. They said they would go to the compound, and we would all catch up there. It will be a good chance to introduce them to Keleli and Sarlith too."

I smiled and nodded. "That's if the two of them are mine."

"I reckon they are. Keleli is like your twin; he looks so much like you. Sarlith, not as much, but I can still tell she is yours."

"Hopefully, the DNA test results will be in soon," I said just as Jericho's phone buzzed. He glanced down and chuckled.

"Hello, Merza; we were just talking about the DNA results," Jericho said.

Merza's laugh tinkled through the speaker. "I must be a witch and know these things or something," she laughed.

Jericho chuckled. "Does that mean you have the results?"

"I sure do. Is Flame there?"

"Yes, I'm here, Merza."

"Excellent. So, the DNA test results show that Keleli and Sarlith are indeed your children. As are all the other children."

"Wait, what? That can't be. I was only pregnant twice," I said with shock. How could that be possible?

"Yes. That's why it took so long to come back because I sent them to be tested again; I thought the lab had made a mistake. But there was no mistake. All the children are yours. They have a different biological father or sperm donor, but they all came from your eggs."

I scrubbed my hand up over my face. It didn't make any sense. "Do all of the children have different sperm donors?" Jericho asked.

"Only Keleli and Sarlith are full siblings. The rest all show a different parentage; the only thing in common is they came from Flame."

"No wonder Ettore didn't want to let you go," Jericho said as he rubbed his hand up and down my spine.

"Yeah," I said with a sigh. "I don't know what any of this means now. I mean, I just don't understand how this is at all possible. I was under the belief that all the omegas other than me conceived through being raped. But if all the children share my egg, they must be implanted."

"Yes. I've spoken to a couple of the omegas, and they said they were implanted. From what I can tell, the ones given to alphas to be impregnated produced omega children. Those children, however, weren't kept."

"Where are they?" I asked.

"The alpha said that Ettore would take them and place them in different facilities. Once they became old enough, they would be impregnated. He said they were also tested and used as guinea pigs for Ettore's scientists to develop stronger alphas."

"Christ," Jericho spat. My heart ached at the thought of what the omega children must have gone through. In one sense, I was lucky that I'd given birth to alphas. At least they had a shot at life. The omega children were basically left to rot.

"So, what happens now?" I asked.

"This is the dilemma we are facing," Merza explained. "Because technically you are the biological parent of all the children, the other omegas don't have the same legal rights. Only you do as the biological parent. If you wanted to give up that right, then the other omegas would be able to adopt the children. However, unless you wanted to give up that right, the children would have to come and live with you."

"Oh. That's not something I think I could do. Having that many children living with me. I'm not sure I want to do that. Is there a way to tell which child was birthed by which omega?"

"No," Merza answered. "We can only tell biologically who made the children; we can't get further than that."

"Alright. I will have to spend a little time thinking about this."

"That's understandable. This is a big shock to everyone. I certainly didn't expect to find out that you had fathered all the children, so I can imagine how shocking this is to you."

"Yeah, it's that. I'll think about it and then get back to you. Is that alright?" I asked as I bit into my bottom lip. The thought of taking on twelve children was too much to think about. I didn't know how to be a parent to one, let alone twelve.

It made me wonder why Ettore had chosen me. Why my eggs? Why me?

"That's not a problem at all. The children are safe with the Devil's Advocates now, so take all the time you need to decide."

"Thank you, Merza. For everything."

"Anytime," she said before ending the call. Jericho looked at me with wide eyes. I shrugged my shoulders.

"Do you know what you'd like to do?"

I shook my head. "I don't know. I feel guilty if I was only to take Keleli and Sarlith. But then, in another sense, I know that twelve children would be far too much for me to handle. Especially now that I'm pregnant. That would be thirteen children in a matter of months."

Jericho nodded before circling his arms around my waist and gently kissing me. "No matter what you decide. I'm going to support you."

I looked up at my mate and smiled. "Thank you. I'm falling in love with you so quickly."

Jericho's face lit up with a bright smile. "I love you too."

Chapter Twenty

J ericho

Flame was quiet after Merza's phone call. I could see that he was trying to work everything out in his mind. I wished I could help him further, but there wasn't anything I could do to change it. This was to be his decision. I would support him if he wanted to take custody of all twelve kids. We'd have to move from the house, but I know that we would be able to do it.

"What are you thinking?" I asked as we drove out towards the Devil's Advocates compound.

Flame sighed. "I'm honestly so confused and not sure what would be best. In one sense, I could see the benefits of the children coming to live with us. But then, while it isn't fair to the omegas who birthed them. I wish there was a way to tell who birthed which child."

I hummed in my throat. "Maybe Iver can tell."

Flame's eyes widened, and he turned in the seat beside me. "Do you think?"

I shrugged my shoulders. "It's worth finding out."

Flame smiled and nodded his head. "I'd be much happier if the omegas that birthed the children could keep the children. They feel like they are more theirs than mine. I know it was my eggs, but I didn't grow them. Does that make sense?"

I nodded my head. "Yes. Complete sense. You don't have the same bond the other omegas would have with the children."

"Exactly," Flame sighed. "Not that I had as much bond with Keleli and Sarlith as I do with this one. I never felt strongly for them because I knew I wouldn't be allowed to keep them. I feel guilty about it."

I sighed and reached out my hand to clasp his. "You shouldn't feel guilty for something out of your control."

Flame sighed and gave me a small smile. "I know logically I shouldn't, but I can't help it."

"I know, baby." I'd spoken with Marlan the day of the raid and had organized to take my annual leave. I had accrued several months but had decided to take four weeks. It was enough to spend time with Flame and get through the first few weeks of his freedom and pregnancy with him. I turned into the Devil's Advocates compound and slowly drove along the driveway toward the main house.

I pulled up to the main house of the Devil's Advocates compound and smiled as the children chased each other around. Some were shifted, and others were using their powers. Jai and Jasper played among them and taught them.

"I can't believe how easily the children have taken to their freedom," Flame said as he stared out the windscreen.

"They have. I think it helps to have some amazing children for them to learn from."

Flame hummed and looked over at me. "Do you think it's fair to remove the children from here?"

I shrugged my shoulders. "I don't know. What are you thinking?"

"I think that even if I took custody only of Keleli and Sarlith, we would go back to your house. And the children would lose all their friends."

"Would you be interested in moving to the compound? I know that Anghus has some houses left here."

Flame glanced over at me and bit into his bottom lip. "I'd like that. This place is so peaceful, and I feel like it is more than just housing; it's a community."

"That's the way Anghus and Lynx have tried to operate it. They wanted this place to become one giant family home. The people that live here have all come from all sorts of walks of life. A lot of them grew up in facilities like you. Anghus has given them not only a place to live but a family and a purpose."

I meant everything I said. I'd always been in awe of what the Devil's Advocates had built. I'd liked Anghus the minute I met him when he first was mated to Bacchus. But the more I got to know all the Devil's Advocates I couldn't find any negatives. What they did was amazing.

"And you think I would be accepted here?"

I smiled and nodded my head. "Definitely."

"What about you? Would you want to move here?"

I smiled and lifted Flame's knuckles to my lips. "I want to be wherever you are, baby."

Flame smiled and nodded his head. "I think I'd like to move here."

"Then consider it done. I'll speak to Anghus about it."

"Thank you."

Chapter Twenty-One

F lame
I spent a lot of time with Keleli and Sarlith, getting to know them. My head was still muddled over what to do with the other children. But the more I got to know the omegas that had been rescued and the children, the more strongly I felt about not taking custody of them. It wasn't anything about the children, but I could start seeing the bonds forming between them and the children. Iver had been able to tell us which child had been birthed by which omega.

I was getting more and more excited about my pregnancy. We hadn't heard anything from Ettore, and I was starting to believe that maybe I was free. Jericho and I had spoken at length with Anghus, and we had found a home on the compound to move into. It helped us to have all the Devil's Advocates, Lalbert fire, and Rigby brothers help move the furniture from Jericho's home. It only took an afternoon, and we were completely moved in.

I wasn't sure what Jericho planned to do with his home now that we wouldn't be living there. I was just excited to be starting my new life. It felt strange to be free to leave the property whenever I felt like it. There was so much available to us on the Devil's Advocates compound. I loved getting in the garden and helping Trudy with growing vegetables. Vaughan, a member of the Devil's Advocates and a troll, farmed pigs, chickens, and even two cows. He'd taught me how to milk a cow and where to collect eggs from. I loved everything that I was learning.

Everyone I'd met was beautiful, and I could see how the Devil's Advocates had managed to grow so big. They really were like a big family. The children were always so happy. I'd even sat in with some of their lessons. It was amazing to watch them learn how to use their powers. I was so proud of Keleli and Sarlith and how easily they managed to join the group.

"Are you ready for your scan?" Larissa asked as we walked back from the dining room towards my home.

I smiled and nodded my head. Larissa had been looking after my pregnancy. She was a nurse and ran the medical unit at the compound.

"I can't wait."

"Are you going to find out what gender you're having?"

I nodded my head. Jericho and I had discussed it already, and he told me that he couldn't wait; he was too impatient. I'd teased him that he was like a little kid before Christmas. Of course, he'd agreed. But I was just as eager. I couldn't wait to find out, either.

"What do you think you're having?" Larissa asked.

"I think we have a girl, but Jericho thinks a boy. I don't know if he asked Iver or not," I said with a laugh.

Larissa threw her head back and laughed. "Well, I guess you'll be able to find out if he cheated or not today."

I grinned and nodded. "Papa," Keleli called. I saw my son and daughter racing toward me with broad smiles.

"Daddy said we were going to the doctor with you to see our baby," Sarlith grinned.

I loved that the children called Jericho Daddy; it was like they had taken to the changes so quickly. I'd overheard them talking about how happy they were when we first moved into the new house. Sarlith had asked Keleli whether he would call Jericho Daddy or Jericho. Keleli was sure that Jericho was now their dad. It made me so happy.

"We are. Are you excited?" I asked.

Sarlith looked up at me with a bright smile and nodded her head. Both children were so happy. Their life in the facility hadn't seemed to affect them negatively at all. We still had regular appointments with Alexandria, the psychiatrist who worked with the Devil's Advocates. I saw her too. She had helped a lot with healing over past traumas.

Jericho came out of the main house and jogged down the stairs toward us. Keleli ran into Jericho's arms, and he swung the boy up onto his shoulders.

"Ready, baby?" he asked.

I grinned and nodded my head. Larissa laughed and leaned over, kissing Sarlith on the top of the head. That was the other thing I'd noticed about the Devil's Advocates. They were all affectionate Everyone was ready to give you a hug or a pat on the back if you needed it.

My life looked very different, and my future looked so much brighter.

Chapter Twenty-Two

J ericho

I was so excited about seeing my baby on the screen. Mama had almost deafened me on the phone with her screams of excitement when I told her. We planned a big weekend get-together so that all of my brothers and their mates could meet Flame, Keleli, and Sarlith.

"Come on through, Jericho and Flame," Reagan called. We all stood and followed Reagan into the ultrasound room. I'd been so excited for this day; the only thing that would top it was when the time came for Flame to give birth.

It was funny to think about who I was before I met Flame. I wasn't someone that cared about whether I met my mate or if I had kids. Thoughts like that were the farthest from my mind. I wasn't interested. All I cared about was my work.

Now though, I had a mate; I had two children and another on the way. I was working with a social worker Michael who had helped in a few cases to officially adopt Keleli and Sarlith. I wanted their names on paper that they were mine. It was strange how protective I already felt for them. It was as if they came from my own biology.

"Alright, Flame, lay up on the bed, and we will have a look at the baby," Reagan instructed.

Jericho lay on the bed while I sat on a chair beside him and pulled Keleli and Sarlith onto my knees.

"This is the gel I'm going to squirt on your belly to make it easier to see the baby; it just helps the wand glide over you. This won't hurt at all," Reagan explained.

"Okay," Flame said as he slowly blew out a breath.

Reagan squirted some gel onto Flame's stomach and moved the wand over. It all looked like a blob on the small television, but I thought I could make out a fetus shape amongst it all.

"Okay, see this little flicker here?" Reagan said, pointing to the screen where the light flashed over and over. "That's your baby's heartbeat, and they look solid."

"Wow," Keleli gasped. "That's our baby."

Reagan chuckled and nodded her head. "Sure is. And these are their arms, and see their legs here."

"Do you know if the baby is a boy or a girl?" Flame asked.

"I will be able to tell you, I'll just grab some measurements, and then I'll be able to tell you."

Reagan went through all the checks she needed to do before humming as she skimmed the wand down over Flame's belly.

She chuckled and shook her head. "The baby is shy," she said with a laugh. "Come on, bubba, move over so I can get a look. Ah, there we go. Okay, you are having a little boy."

I grinned as Keleli and Sarlith both roared with excitement. "We are getting a brother Sarlith," Keleli crowed.

Sarlith grinned and bounced her head up and down. I didn't think it mattered what gender the baby was. They would have been overly excited. They were just thrilled to have a sibling.

I glanced over at Flame, who was watching us with a smile. "A boy," he gushed.

I leaned forward and pressed a kiss to Flame's lips. "A boy."

Flame pulled back and narrowed his eyes. "Wait. Did you ask Iver?"

I threw my head back and laughed, shaking my head. "No. I was tempted, but I didn't."

Reagan laughed. "Well, now that you know you're having a boy, you will be able to ask Iver what supernatural you are having."

"I don't mind what supernatural they are; I didn't even mind what gender I was having," Flame said with a sigh. "I just want a healthy baby."

"You are having a healthy baby. Everything looks perfect; his size is great, so your dates are spot on."

"That's fantastic news," I said with a smile.

I couldn't wait to share the news with my family. I knew that Burgess and March would be all over designing a nursery for our son. My life just kept getting better and better.

Chapter Twenty-Three

Flame

"I can't wait to meet your family," I gushed to Jericho as I put the last salads on the table, ready for the Rigby family's arrival. I'd already met Bacchus and Obsidian, and if they were all like them, I knew I'd get along with them well.

The doorbell rang. "You don't have long to wait," Jericho chuckled as he went to answer the door.

"Jericho," a woman's voice said. I entered the living room where Keleli and Sarlith sat, coloring in.

"Mama," Jericho said as he hugged his Mama and brought her into the living room. "This is my mate, Flame, and our children, Keleli and Sarlith."

"Oh, my gracious, they are so beautiful," she said with tears in her eyes.

"This is my Mama, Abigail, and my Papa, Lionel."

"It's great to meet you both," I said.

Abigail walked towards me and pulled me into her arms in a tight hug. "Welcome to the family, Flame."

I smiled and looked into Abigail's face. Jericho was right. She was so warm and welcoming. It didn't matter what my life was before; she was prepared to accept both of us. Abigail let go of me and went to where Keleli and Sarlith were sitting on the floor.

"I have brought you a present to welcome you to the family," she said as she climbed onto the floor beside my children.

Keleli and Sarlith looked over with interest. This was all new to them. In the facility, no children got presents; it just didn't happen. Abigail opened her bag, where she pulled out two teddy bears. She handed one each to the children whose faces lit up. Sarlith held her bear close to her chest.

"These bears are special; they used to belong to your Daddy when he was a young boy," Abigail said.

Keleli's eyes lit up, and he glanced over at Jericho. "Will the baby get one when he is born?"

Abigail chuckled and nodded her head. "Yes. I have a special one for baby brother when he arrives."

Keleli smiled and hugged the bear tight. "It smells like Daddy," he said quietly.

Abigail smiled and nodded her head. "I always knew that he would have children to share them with one day. I'm glad that I finally get to see that day."

My eyes were welled with tears. I couldn't believe that this was my life. I'd come from so much shit, and now I was welcomed and loved. I had a family. My children had a family. Hell, I even had children. We'd only been together for a month, but it felt like so much had happened in that month. In a sense, I guess it really had.

The door opened, and more loud voices floated into the room. It wasn't long before the house was full of Rigby's and their children. The kids all embraced Keleli and Sarlith like one of their own. Looking at the children, you'd never guess that they had only just met Keleli and Sarlith. However, I shouldn't have been surprised. The kids were led by Iver, and that boy was something special.

"So, what are you thinking for the nursery?" Burgess asked. I was sitting beside him and March outside in the shade of one of the large trees that loomed over the backyard.

"I don't know, really. I honestly hadn't given it much thought beyond what furniture we would need," I responded.

"That's okay. Did Jericho ask you whether you would like us to decorate?" March asked.

I nodded my head. Jericho said that Burgess and March loved to do all the nursery artwork; I was thrilled with the idea but wasn't sure what I wanted to do. "He did, and I love the idea. I just don't know what I want exactly. I know I want something fantasy, something that goes beyond the realm of reality."

"A cave, Papa," Sarlith said from behind me. I turned in my seat, not knowing my daughter had been there.

"A cave?" I asked.

Sarlith nodded her head. "The baby's room. It should be a cave with glow worms and colorful mushrooms."

My eyes widened, and I gasped. It was perfect; looking over at Burgess and March, I saw they felt the same way.

"Consider it done," March said with a grin before turning to Sarlith. "Now, little lady, what would you like for your room?"

Sarlith hummed and tapped her finger on her chin in thought. "I want sunflowers. I want to feel like I'm sleeping in a field of sunflowers."

I had no idea where she got her thoughts, but I loved the idea. "That sounds perfect. We will have to ask Keleli what he would like," I said.

Sarlith nodded her head. "I bet he will want a dragon's lair."

My eyes widened. "How do you know what a dragon's lair is?"

Sarlith giggled. "It's in our book that we are reading at school."

I smiled and leaned over, kissing my daughter's cheek. All too soon, though, commotion drew my attention. The backyard suddenly flooded with other Devils. Anghus and Bacchus were on their phones barking orders. Iver looked like he was having a silent conversation with someone.

"What's going on?" I asked, feeling fear start to ricochet through my chest.

"Baby, pack the kids up; we need to get you all to the AJE authority," Jericho shouted.

"What's going on," I said, feeling my panic overwhelm me.

"Ettore, he's taken another child."

My eyes widened, and I gasped. "Which child? From where?"

"One of the Onyx Rebel's children, Wrennyn. Hawke and Jabari's child."

"A demon," I gasped, remembering the child with dark hair and black eyes. I placed them because Jabari explained how Wrennyn was born without a gender. Making them powerful demons.

"Everyone, stop," Iver shouted.

We all turned our attention to the teen as he stood in the middle of the backyard. "Wrennyn is going to be safe. They have been taken to the underworld, but Hel is going there; she is going to protect Wrennyn. Lilith is coming out of hiding. The underworld is about to be shaken up."

I looked at Jericho with wide eyes. This could only mean one thing. The war was on our doorstep. It was closer than we first thought. I stroked my hand down over my belly. My baby would be born into a war. But I would fight. I would fight with everything I had. I wasn't going to let Ettore win this one.

E ttore
   "I want to go home," the child sniveled. I rolled my eyes and sighed. I didn't know how many times the child would grizzle at me. It was the same thing.

"Well, I've got news for you, kid, you aren't going home. You are here to stay. Two of my children betrayed me; I will ensure one of theirs betrays them."

Once Alrick, my son, came and helped destroy my facility, I knew what I would do. It hadn't been in my plan to take the child, but after the AJE authority had come and destroyed my facility and taken all the omegas, I made the snap decision. I couldn't get to Iver, but I'd go to the second most powerful. The one that they didn't think I knew about. Silent tears fell down the child's cheeks.

I'd been on the defensive since they'd shut down my Siberian facility. But that was all going to change. I was going to bring this to an end.

"Ettore," Blaise Knight said as he came into the room where I was standing with the child who hadn't stopped crying.

I turned and smiled at the man closest to being a friend. I didn't have friends. I had people I tolerated and trusted more than others. But honestly, no one had my trust.

"Lilith is outside."

My eyes widened. Well, this was a turn-up for the books. I hadn't expected to see that cunt back. I straightened and set my jaw. Turning on my heel, I stormed out of the room and to the courtyard, where demons stood watching in awe. Lilith. I hadn't seen her in thousands of years. Yet she was still as beautiful as when I first met her.

My heart ached. The one woman I'd ever loved. But she never returned that love to me. I clenched my jaw and narrowed my eyes to glare.

"What's this? Decided after all this time you would come back?"

Lilith curled her lip in a sneer. "Give the child back, Ettore."

I chuckled and shook my head. "What child would that be?"

Lilith rolled her eyes and crossed her arms across her chest. "You know very well what child I'm referring to. That child is innocent."

"That child is a demon. They belong here in the underworld. Or have you forgotten Hel's promise that she made to the earth dwellers? Demons would stay in the underworld."

Lilith snorted and shook her head. "And you have walked all over that rule, haven't you? How many demons are on earth? How many have you crossed over?"

I smirked. She wasn't wrong. I'd been flaunting that law for years. I had a good thing going with the demon council. They turned a blind eye, and I gave them all the women and wealth they wanted. It worked well for both of us.

"The child is to remain here. They will be trained to be a demon seer."

"This is too far, Ettore. This will bring you down."

I laughed and shrugged my shoulders before leaning further forward. "You and whose army is going to stop me."

Lilith's eyes flared. Stupid bitch. She didn't realize that I would gladly kill her. I would gladly ruin her. I'd just thrown down the gauntlet, and I knew she would happily pick it up. It was going to take the power of the gods to stop me. And even then, they would have to outwit me.

I was going to win this war. I knew they had a prophecy that stated otherwise, but here is the thing about time. It changes. Things change. Plans evolve, and new victors rise. I was going to rule. I was going to win. And there was no human, supernatural, or God on this earth that could change it.

I turned and stormed back into the house. I had something they all wanted. Let them come and fight me for it. A smile caressed my face as

I continued down the halls and toward my private chambers. Opening the door, I breathed in deeply as I closed it behind me. Glancing over to the large bed where the trembling woman lied.

"Ready to produce more, my love," I purred as I stalked towards the bed.

"Please, Ettore, no more," the woman cried.

I chuckled. "You're not a goddess here, Aphrodite."

"Please, it's been so long; surely you can let me go. I gave you sons."

I laughed and shook my head. "Dite, my love, you made a huge mistake when you came all those years ago to dance with the devil. And now you belong to me. Besides, Flame turned his back on me. Turned on me, but don't worry, our grandchild is coming, and that little dragon shifter Sawyer will be mine too. All my children turned their backs. Well, except Rison. He is a good boy. But the others. The others will pay."

Tears trekked down the fallen goddesses' cheeks. My secret weapon. The one that was going to keep me safe. The one that no one knew I had. Captive. For over a millennium. The mother of my children and the one they would never believe I had managed to hold captive and stripped of her powers. A lesson to be learned. Never make deals with the devil; he always expects you to repay.

The End.

Don't miss out!

Visit the website below and you can sign up to receive emails whenever S L Davies publishes a new book. There's no charge and no obligation.

https://books2read.com/r/B-A-NZRR-QIQBC

BOOKS 2 READ

Connecting independent readers to independent writers.

Did you love *Jericho*? Then you should read *Breeding Facility*[1] by S L Davies!

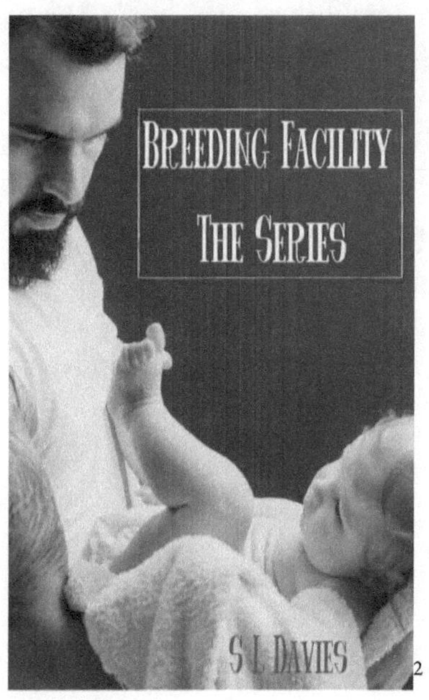

[2]

All in one book is the Breeding Facility Series.

Book One: Memphis

Book Two: Bacchus

Book Three: Coltrane

Book Four: Pax

Book Five: Raiden

Book Six: Nash

Follow the men of the AJE authorities shifter unit as they attempt to shut down the breeding facilities run by the notoriously evil group Morpheus. This contains triggering subjects that may offend some readers. Language and themes suited to 18+

---

1. https://books2read.com/u/4jq5VD

2. https://books2read.com/u/4jq5VD

Also by S L Davies

Breeding Facility
Memphis
Bacchus
Coltrane
Pax
Raiden
Nash
Breeding Facility

Devil's Advocates
Lynx
Israel
Jai
Jasper
Arley
Zion
Oakland

KINK
Gunner

Newlyn
Freya
Tanquil

Obsidian Mechanics
Donte
Atticus

Onyx Rebels
Onyx Rebels Prologue
Hawke
Rison
Bandit
Butler

Rigby Brothers
Asher
Burgess
Macklin
Drake
Jericho
Obsidian

Schiavu
Schiavu

Shifter Ink
Brenton
Chase
Orion

Stolen
Stolen
The Murphy Princess
Little Warrior

Standalone
Sisters Revenge
Killer Love
Soldiers At War
Second Chances
Bunny
Caged
By The Sword
The Cult
Rising Sun

About the Author

S L Davies is an Australian Author living in Country, Victoria. She is inspired by the world around her.

Read more at https://www.amazon.com/~/e/B0832T8F7Z.